CAPTAIN COOK

Oliver Warner

HORIZON • NEW WORD CITY

Published by New Word City, Inc.

For more information about New Word City, visit our Web site at NewWordCity.com

Copyright © 2016 by American Heritage Publishing.
All rights reserved.

American Heritage Publishing
Edwin S. Grosvenor, President
P.O. Box 1488
Rockville, MD 20851

American Heritage and the eagle logo are registered trademarks of American Heritage Publishing, and used pursuant to a license agreement.

No part of this book may be reproduced, stored in a retrieval system, or transmitted in any form or by any means, electronic, mechanical, photocopying, recording, scanning, or otherwise except as permitted under Section 107 or 108 of the 1976 United States Copyright Act, without the prior written permission of American Heritage Publishing.

Requests for permission should be addressed to the Permissions Department, American Heritage Publishing, Box 1488, Rockville, MD 20849 (email: licenses@americanheritage.com).

Permission for certain uses of this book can also be obtained at Copyright.com, or by mail or phone to Copyright Clearance Center, 222 Rosewood Drive, Danvers, MA 01923, (978) 750-8400.

1
THE MAPMAKER 5

2
ENDEAVOR 29

3
SECRET ORDERS 55

4
RESOLUTION 79

5
POLYNESIAN ADVENTURERS 113

6
A NORTHERN PASSAGE 125

SOURCES 163

1
THE MAPMAKER

James Cook once described himself as a man "who had ambition not only to go farther than anyone had done before but as far as possible for man to go . . ." These words not only sum up his professional aspirations but also give a rare, personal glimpse of the man himself.

Cook had a piercing curiosity, but he was no visionary seafarer like his great predecessor Ferdinand Magellan. Cook was a methodical explorer with the soul of a scientist. He was born into an age when the search for scientific knowledge was as intense as the thirst for conquest had once been.

By the 1700s, England, eager to expand its empire, was sending exploring parties to all the corners of the then-known globe, and the most daring into the still unknown. The eighteenth century, the age of reason and enlightenment, required a new kind of explorer: not a rover or a plunderer, or a seeker of adventure for its own sake, but a master of navigation and seamanship. An explorer was expected to be a skilled surveyor and chart maker, with natural curiosity and a flair for command. Cook was that man.

He was born on October 27, 1728, in a two-room clay cottage in the remote Yorkshire village of Marton. His father, also named James, was a day laborer who did such odd jobs as slopping hogs. On one of his jobs, he met Grace Pace, who was eight years younger. Four months after they were married, she gave birth to their first son, John.

James, the second of eight children, was a bright youngster, so much so that his father's employer financed his early schooling. James's father had been promoted to foreman at the largest farm in the region. Young James, like other sons of farmers, was expected to follow in his father's footsteps.

But James rebelled as a boy, preferring solitude to the bustle of the farm. He often wandered off to explore the wilderness around it - collecting specimens, particularly birds' nests, which fascinated him with their intricate structure. From an early age, James Cook had a restless spirit that refused to be confined and longed to range free.

At school, his instructors saw him as a charismatic loner with "a steady adherence to his own schemes," but also "something in his manners and deportment which attracted the reverence and respect of his companions."

As he grew older, James worked on the farm with his father, though he quickly realized there was no future in it for him. He looked up to some of the men on the farm - including its owner, Thomas Skottowe, who was paying for his schooling - and never forgot the work ethic he learned there. But in 1745, when his formal education ended, James was ready to set out on his own path.

His father found him a job with a shopkeeper in Staithes, a tiny fishing village northwest of Whitby. He spent most days stocking shelves and weighing fish. The fishermen who came into the shop regularly told stories about their adventures in the North Sea, and young James craned his neck to listen. At night, James slept under the shop's counter. By candlelight, he pored over books he had stacked there - on geography, astronomy, and mathematics - and dreamed about far-off realms.

The shop was close to the sea, within sight of ships sailing to and from the nearby port of Whitby, and within earshot of surf pounding the rocky shore. It was here that James developed his lifelong love of the sea, spending summers on the water and winters learning the shipwright's craft.

Cook's preference for seafaring was obvious to everyone. In September 1746, his employer at the shop graciously arranged for him to interview with a shipping firm owned by John and Henry Walker.

The Walkers were prominent coal shippers who ran coal-carrying vessels, called colliers, between London and the Yorkshire towns along the North Sea coast. At the time, Whitby was a coastal-trade center as well as an important shipbuilding site. Cook arrived flush and tired after hiking, with all of his belongings in a pack slung over his shoulder, about a dozen miles along a trail that skirted the rugged coastline. He rushed to the waterfront to gaze out at the armada of cargo ships - many from foreign ports with crews that came ashore speaking unfamiliar languages. From Whitby, he realized, it would be easy enough to fulfill his desire to roam.

Cook entered John Walker's office and asked for a job. Though more than six feet tall, Cook had a fresh face and awkward innocence that worried Walker. The boy seemed a stark contrast to the hardened and weathered sailors in Walker's outfit. Impressed by Cook's eagerness to learn, however, Walker decided to hire him as an apprentice - though seventeen generally was considered too old to begin an apprenticeship and Cook was nearly eighteen.

Cook reported to his first ship, the collier *Freelove*. While docked, he learned the menial jobs assigned to all young ship hands: swabbing the deck, polishing the hull, and cleaning the latrines. He also came to grasp the names and purposes of the various ropes, knots, and sails that would be essential on the open sea. He was issued a hammock that he hung in the ship's hold - next to those of other apprentices, with whom he was now competing for advancement.

Before the year was out, Cook was at sea on his first voyage, hauling coal along the British coast. For each of the next three years of his apprenticeship, he made at least a dozen such voyages. He transferred to another of Walker's ships, the *Three Brothers*, and then others. Quickly, he learned to handle the awkward but capable colliers and sail them safely in dangerous waters. Soon he was sailing on open-ocean passages across the North Sea. When not at sea he studied math and astronomy. Cook served nine years in the North Sea trade, earning promotions to able seaman, mate, and then second-in-command of his ship for the last three years.

He learned to trust his instincts. Coastal charts were unreliable, and a seaman needed a sixth sense to protect his ship from shoals, sandbanks, and changes of current. Cook was unusually perceptive. He gained a reputation for sailing where other navigators dared not go; he seemed to know instinctively which waters were safest. His officers often said that he could smell land; he would appear suddenly on deck and alter his ship's course when no one else was aware that there was danger of running aground.

Cook served the Walkers of Whitby so well that in 1755 he was offered command of one of their colliers - the best and largest ship in the fleet, the *Friendship*. But at twenty-seven years old, he wanted a change. England was mobilizing its forces in preparation for war with France, and its navy was desperate for recruits. Cook recognized the need for experienced seamen, and at the same time, saw the possibility of advancing his career at sea. He rejected Walker's offer, saying he intended to join the Royal Navy.

In his jaunts to London, on coal business, Cook had seen Royal Navy officers - in their powdered, white wigs, polished shoes, and blue-and-gold uniforms - and their superior vessels. Walker warned Cook that an officer's life was not as glamorous as it might seem: The ranks of the Royal Navy were filled with derelicts, pressed into service, who knew nothing about life at sea, and so were doomed to die there. Many succumbed to disease, the worst culprit being scurvy.

Walker tried other arguments. A Royal Navy officer might be at sea for years before receiving any compensation. But the best reason for staying put, Walker said, was that in Whitby, Cook would be a captain. If he joined the Royal Navy, he would be starting over as an ordinary seaman. Officers were recruited from the upper class, and groomed at a young age. But Cook craved adventure and the distant horizons that could be reached aboard the larger Royal Navy barque. "I want to make my future fortune there," he told Walker as he walked out of his office and away from Whitby.

In the Navy

Cook enlisted as a sailor on one of King George II's warships, the sixty-gun *Eagle*. The ship, first launched in 1745, was 147 feet from stern to bow and 1,130 tons, able to carry a crew of 420 men (ten times what Cook was accustomed to). Its captain, Joseph Hamar, had commanded the HMS *Flamborough*, protecting the coasts of British colonies in South Carolina and Georgia from the Spanish. Now his orders were to patrol the waters south of Ireland and capture French ships. Hamar sized up his crew of mostly green ship hands and decided that none were up to the task. But Cook soon proved the captain wrong.

The officers noticed that Cook looked different from the other new recruits. Besides being older, he had the weathered appearance of a true sailor - a face ruddy from exposure to the sea breeze and large, calloused hands. After testing his knowledge of the ship's rigging, the officers realized Cook would be more useful above deck. There, he displayed an aptitude for navigation that caught the attention of Captain Hamar. Just five weeks after joining the *Eagle*'s crew, Cook was promoted to master's mate - primarily responsible, under his captain, for navigating the ship and keeping the ship's log.

The *Eagle* offered splendid training for a young man eager to learn the business of navigating and scientific surveying. But after just three months, Captain Hamar took the ship back to port for repairs. He was nearing retirement and kept delaying a return to battle, aggravating his superiors, and he was relieved of his command.

Cook was fortunate that the new captain, Hugh Palliser, quickly recognized Cook's abilities and became the young man's patron and friend. Five years older than Cook, Palliser had entered the Royal Navy in 1735, at age twelve, as a midshipman aboard the HMS *Aldborough*, which was commanded by his uncle. By the time he was eighteen, Palliser was a lieutenant, and five years later, was given his first command. The period between 1746 and his arrival on the *Eagle* was filled with the sort of danger and adventure that Cook was eager to experience.

While sailing in the West Indies in 1748, Palliser was wounded when an ammunition chest caught fire and exploded, sending shots flying that killed two other men. He returned to duty despite a lame left leg and sometimes excruciating pain. He sailed to the East Indies, and then was assigned to a ship guarding the Royal Navy dockyard at Chatham, on England's southeast coast.

On his most recent mission to the colonies, Palliser sailed far south of the usual route. He reached as far as the Tropic of Cancer, a line of latitude about twenty-three degrees north of the Equator, a route that avoided most of the storms and turbulent waters that caused problems for ships crossing the North Sea. This confirmed his reputation as a brilliant seaman and tactician.

Captain Palliser won Cook's immediate respect, and before long, the feeling was mutual. Palliser taught his first mate all he knew about seamanship and navigation, including the surveying and charting of coastlines and bodies of water. For Cook, the relationship with Palliser was one of the most formative of his life. Later, Palliser would play a significant role in promoting Cook's work as a mapmaker and sponsoring his famed explorations. In return, Cook would name several of his discoveries in honor of his "worthy friend."

In October 1755, Captain Palliser wasted no time in getting the *Eagle* back out to sea. War had officially broken out between England and France - later, it would become known as the Seven Years' War - and so far, it had not gone well for the British. An expedition by General Edward Braddock to reinforce the American colonies had ended disastrously, with Braddock's death and the

French gaining momentum. In London, this news led to a public outcry over the government's poor military preparation. Britain needed a victory, and Palliser was determined to provide one.

Patrolling the western entrance to the English Channel, separating southern England from northern France, the *Eagle* plunged into battle on November 15 with the French ship *Espérance*. It was the first action that Cook had seen since joining the Royal Navy, and he did not play a large part. But he was thrilled by the fight, which after three hours succeeded in sinking the *Espérance*.

The *Eagle* did not see battle again until a year and a half later. On May 30, 1757, as the ship turned back toward England, it encountered the fifty-gun French frigate *Duc d'Aquitain* off the island of Ushant. The *Duc d'Aquitain* was much larger than the *Espérance*, and its crew fought ferociously. Luckily, the *Eagle* was reinforced by another British ship, the sixty-gun *Medway*. The battle resulted in eighty of Cook's crewmates being wounded and ten killed, while on the French crew, fifty were killed and thirty wounded before the *Duc d'Aquitaine* surrendered. Captain Palliser wrote in his ship's log: "We engaged about three-quarters of an hour at point-blank range."

The *Eagle* was damaged badly in the fight, but the Admiralty was pleased with the outcome. Though Cook's role in the victory was minor, he shared in the prize money, and Palliser recommended his promotion to ship master. On June 29, 1757, Cook passed a difficult written and oral examination to earn his master's warrant. The next morning, he was assigned to the twenty-four-gun frigate *Solebay*, based near Edinburgh in Scotland.

The trip overland from London to Scotland allowed Cook to stop briefly in Whitby and then Ayton – and to update his former employer, John Walker, and father on his accomplishments, which happily won their approval. But Cook served only two months on the *Solebay* before being transferred again.

On his twenty-ninth birthday, he joined the crew of the sixty-four-gun *Pembroke* as master, under Captain John Simcoe. Simcoe had a reputation for being a well-read and intellectual officer, skilled in mathematics and curious about science. He always sailed with a small library, which he made available to Cook. He encouraged Cook to read English professor Charles Leadbetter's treatises on mathematics and astronomy. So Cook's education continued aboard the *Pembroke*. But, more than a classroom, the *Pembroke* was a warship, and Simcoe a fighting captain.

Cook's first mission aboard the *Pembroke* was to patrol the Bay of Biscay and then to blockade the western coast of France. The *Pembroke* was part of a fleet, under the command of Admiral Edward

Boscawen, ordered to sail to North America and attack French vessels and ports in Canada in 1758. It would be the farthest that Cook had ever sailed and also his first encounter with scurvy.

By the time the *Pembroke* reached the British base of Halifax, Nova Scotia, twenty-six of the crew had died of scurvy. Many more were gravely ill. The *Pembroke* had to stay behind while the crew recovered when the rest of the fleet sailed on. Cook watched wistfully as an armada of 157 British warships left the harbor.

The fleet was to take part in the siege of Louisbourg, a fortress on the eastern tip of Nova Scotia. The English considered Louisbourg a strategic objective because it commanded the Gulf of St. Lawrence at the mouth of the river. While the French held Louisbourg, no attack on the capital of New France - the city of Quebec - was possible.

By the time the *Pembroke* finally sailed from Nova Scotia in June, the siege was already underway. An English infantry force had attacked the fortress at Louisbourg. A choppy sea made the landing difficult, and many soldiers drowned. Still others were slaughtered by the raking French gunfire. But the determined English refused to retreat. Luckily for the British, French reinforcements, also depleted by the spread of disease at sea, never arrived.

The *Pembroke* caught up to the fleet just in time to take part in the last major battle. Sailing into a dense fog, Captain Simcoe and Master Cook led an assault on two French warships, capturing one and burning the other. The next day, the French surrendered Louisbourg.

Now the only deterrent to an attack on Quebec was the St. Lawrence River, choked with shoals and dangerous reefs. Cook and the masters of a few other vessels were asked to chart a suitable route through the narrow channel. If their work proved accurate, the English fleet could sail through the channel and anchor opposite the city.

Cook had studied charts but had no experience creating them. After the fall of Louisbourg, Cook was walking on shore when he spotted an army lieutenant and engineer named Samuel Holland, seated at a surveyor's plane table – a small, square surface mounted on a tripod - making a drawing of the coastline. Holland recognized that Cook was taking a keen interest in his work, and offered to give him lessons.

When Cook reported this to his captain, Simcoe gave his consent for the lessons and said he would join them. Captain Simcoe was ill and unable to leave his ship, so surveying lessons took place aboard the *Pembroke*. Holland taught Cook and Simcoe the technique of triangulation using the plane table and a device called an alidade, an eyepiece which is rotated and swiveled to measure angles and distance of objects.

Holland, a Dutchman, had emigrated from the Netherlands to England in 1754, leaving his wife behind, to try to advance his career. He had much in common with Cook; they were the same age and had similar ambitions, and both were confident and reliable. Before Louisbourg, Holland had created a map of England's New York province that would be widely used for twenty years. But nothing he had accomplished before was as immediately critical as the survey of the St. Lawrence, which would determine the success or failure of the British invasion of Quebec.

This was extremely hazardous duty for Holland, Cook, and the other surveyors. It required them to row out in small boats - individually, unprotected, and with nothing but their surveying equipment - to gauge currents, calculate depths, and locate the sand bars and rocky shoals that might impede the larger warships. Much of the time, they made their soundings under the noses of the French, because Quebec's main fortifications stood atop an enormous promontory that overlooked the channel. Cook went about his work calmly and efficiently, even though the threat of death or capture was literally hanging over his head.

The surveyors used French charts, captured at Louisbourg, as reference, but all were outdated or simply inaccurate. Cook's chart would set a new mark for detail and accuracy. On it, he noted the latitude (but not longitude), scale in miles, magnetic variations, many soundings, tidal range and direction, and provided two horizontal views of the coast. Charting a suitable course took several months to complete, during which tragedy struck the *Pembroke*.

On May 15, 1759, Captain Simcoe, who had been sick for some time, died aboard his ship. Asked during his final, lucid moments if his body should be preserved for burial ashore, Simcoe said: "Apply your pitch to its proper purpose, keep your lead to mend the shot holes, and commit me to the deep." Two days later, Simcoe's body was laid to rest in the mouth of the St. Lawrence River, off the coast of Anticosti Island, as the *Pembroke* boomed a twenty-one-gun salute.

Command of the Pembroke now passed to Captain John Wheelock, Cook's fifth captain in four years and the one who made the least impression. In June 1759, Wheelock gave the order to sail ahead of a huge fleet - more than 100 ships - to begin the siege on Quebec.

On the Pembroke, Cook took more soundings of the channel and guided the fleet through a particularly narrow and treacherous section known as "the Traverse." The French tried to block the passage by sending seven ships, which they set ablaze, but British sailors in longboats were able to haul the fire ships out of the fleet's path. The Pembroke was one of the first ships to anchor at Quebec's Île d'Orléans on June 28. Soon after, the British fleet poured soldiers onto the shore, and the battle began.

After more than six weeks of fighting, the French surrendered Quebec to the British on September 18, 1760. The victory was a major turning point in the war between England and France - and established England as the dominant power in North America. When the Seven Years' War ended three years later, the Treaty of Paris would award Britain parts of New France, including Canada.

Cook's role in the victory was not overlooked. On September 23, he received news that he was being promoted again, this time to master of the flagship *Northumberland*. Now, Cook undertook his first important piece of independent work: a detailed survey of the St. Lawrence River from Quebec to the Atlantic Ocean. Cook's meticulous charts made earlier ones obsolete and firmly established his reputation as a skilled marine surveyor.

Winter soon set in, and pack ice began to close the mouth of the river. The British fleet had to sail away from Quebec or risk being trapped there for months. This was Cook's first experience at navigating through icy waters, but certainly not the last.

Cook returned to the British base at Halifax, Nova Scotia, where he spent much of the next two years surveying and supervising improvements to the Navy Yard and harbor. This work included the construction of several buildings, including a mast house for shipbuilding and repairs. At night, he slept in the master's cabin on the *Northumberland*, and by candlelight, continued his education. He found a Halifax bookseller who stocked "a large and curious Collection of Books, in History, Divinity, Law, Physics, Mathematics, Classics, Architecture, Navigation," as well as maps and charts of Nova Scotia, New England, and more. So, while his crewmates were out getting drunk on rum, Cook most often was nose-deep in a book.

Though he served for three years on the *Northumberland*, Cook did not fight in another sea battle. On October 7, 1762, he sailed east, and nineteen days later, landed home at England for the first time in nearly five years.

"Great Encouragement to New Adventures"

Back in London, Cook was relieved of his duty to the Royal Navy. With the war winding down, England was at peace, and no longer needed so many sailors to fill its fleet. The Navy paid Cook about £300 (equal to about $70,000 today) for his four years of service. At thirty-four years old, Cook wandered the city with, for the first time in his life, full pockets and time to spare. He decided to use it to find a wife.

Just two months later, Cook married twenty-one-year-old Elizabeth Batts, the daughter of a London innkeeper. He used most of his pay from the Navy to buy a three-story brick row house east of the busy heart of London. It was across the street from a pub, next door to a gin mill, and about a mile from the mighty Thames River. Briefly, love-struck Cook considered giving up his life at sea to stay close to Elizabeth. But a large part of what had drawn Elizabeth to him was his adventurous spirit and his dream - which he had told only her - of sailing farther and wider than anyone ever had. Soon, the sea was calling him again, and the house on Mile End Road became little more than a place to rest between voyages.

Elizabeth accepted her role of abandoned wife with grace and resolution. Though in eleven years of marriage, they were often apart for years at a time, their love for one another endured. James was absent, thousands of miles at sea, for the births of most of their six children. He wrote his wife many letters, which he mailed at every major port. And despite outliving him by more than six decades, Elizabeth never remarried.

The Royal Navy recalled Cook just a few months after the wedding, in the spring of 1763. After the signing of the Treaty of Paris, King George III needed a mapmaker to chart his new territories. Cook's former captain, Lord Alexander Colville, recommended him to the Admiralty, writing: "From my experience of Mr. Cook's genius and capacity, I think him well qualified for the work he had performed and for greater undertakings of the same kind. These Draughts being made under my own Eye I can venture to say they may be the means of directing many in the right way, but cannot mislead any." The Admiralty was impressed with Cook's charts and drawings from Nova Scotia, as well as his work with Samuel Holland to chart Quebec's St. Lawrence River.

Cook was summoned and offered the handsome salary of ten shillings a day to be the king's surveyor. It was the same salary that Hugh Palliser had been paid as captain of the *Eagle*. Cook's first assignment was to map the unknown coast of Newfoundland and the nearby islands of St. Pierre and Miquelon. The islands were to be given back to France, as fishing ports, under the Treaty of Paris. Before that happened, King George wanted to know more about what he was giving up. Under the treaty, the islands could not be fortified.

In April 1763, Cook joined the crew of the *Antelope*, commanded by Thomas Graves, who was to be Britain's governor of Newfoundland. Cook left

Elizabeth behind, pregnant with their first child, and sailed again across the North Sea.

He arrived on the damp, fog-obscured Newfoundland coast at the beginning of June, eager to start his work. Governor Graves provided Cook with a crew and a small schooner, the *Grenville*, which he sailed up and down the 6,000 miles of Newfoundland coastline for the next seven months.

As winter threatened, he sailed back to England, though his work was far from done. The pack ice encroaching the harbor would make his work impossible. Besides, Cook had received the news that his wife had given birth to a son, whom she named James; he was home in time for the baptism. He returned to Newfoundland to continue his survey the following summer, once again leaving behind a pregnant Elizabeth.

His former captain Palliser was now the governor. Palliser arranged for Cook to command a series of chart-making expeditions in Labrador as well as Newfoundland. Cook was grateful for the continued employment in the Royal Navy at a time when scores of sailors were set adrift.

For five years, Cook spent the winters in England completing his charts and summers in Newfoundland. He earned a reputation as an efficient, dedicated, yet coldly scientific individual.

Though he nearly lost all use of his hand in an accident in 1764, Cook continued his chart work with precision. His charts of Newfoundland and Labrador were so accurate that they remained in use until late in the nineteenth century. Governor Palliser wrote to the secretary of the Admiralty that the publication of Cook's charts "will be a great encouragement to new adventures in the fisheries upon these coasts."

One of the few distractions from his survey work was an eclipse of the sun during the summer of 1766. He knew from his studies in astrology that the eclipse was due on August 5, and he waited on his schooner *Grenville* off the Burgeo Islands, southwest of Newfoundland. He sent a detailed report of the eclipse to London, which further enhanced his prestige as a scientist. This report caught the attention of England's leading scientific body, the Royal Society, which now became interested in Cook. That same year, the Royal Society was planning a mission that only a seaman-scientist of Cook's caliber could handle.

2
ENDEAVOR

George III, who came to power in 1760, was just the right sort of monarch for James Cook. The first English monarch to systematically study science, even as a boy he was interested in chemistry, physics, astronomy, mathematics, geography, and agriculture. He opened his collection of books to scholars as The King's Library, which became the foundation of a national library. Most significantly, unlike his predecessors, the new king preferred to extend his imperial authority through exploration rather than conquest.

When the war with France ended, the king sent several explorers to the South Pacific. In 1767, as Cook worked in London to finish his final survey of

Newfoundland, Captain Samuel Wallis was sailing through the Strait of Magellan. Wallis's ship was the twenty-four-gun Royal Navy frigate *Dolphin*, which was making its second circumnavigation of the world; the first was completed in 1766 by Commodore John Byron. In June, Wallis discovered Tahiti, which he named "King George the Third's Island." However, the captain was ill - from dysentery or scurvy - and remained in his cabin. So it was his lieutenant, Tobias Furneaux, who first set foot on the island and planted the flag for England. Captain Wallis survived the expedition, though more than thirty of the *Dolphin*'s crew died from the same illness. His reports and consultations would help to inform and prepare the next great plunge into the Pacific.

The king's selection of James Cook as Wallis's successor was surprising. Most people expected that Alexander Dalrymple, a true scientist and lifelong student of geography and surveying, would lead the next expedition to the Pacific. Dalrymple was writing a manuscript outlining his theory that a southern continent not only existed but extended well north into temperate climates.

This expedition, after all, was envisioned with science as its principal goal. Wallis had not yet returned from the Pacific when the Royal Society proposed to King George a mission to observe a rare astronomical event that would not repeat for more than 100 years.

Earlier in the century, the astronomer Edmund Halley had predicted that in 1769 the planet Venus would pass between the earth and the sun. The last time that had happened was 1761, and the next occurrence would not be until 1874. If this phenomenon, called the transit of Venus, were accurately observed, astronomers thought it might be possible to calculate the exact distance between the earth and the sun. In order to validate the calculations, a committee of the Royal Society suggested that the transit be observed from three different vantage points: Hudson Bay, North Cape (northernmost point of Europe), and an unnamed spot in the South Pacific.

King George agreed to finance the South Pacific expedition to the tune of £4,000 (worth nearly $1 million today) and provide a crew. The Royal Society had its own candidates, with Dalrymple at the top of the list, to command the expedition. But Admiralty policy had changed.

Civilians in the past had failed to exercise strong leadership at sea, with disastrous results. A recent example was Halley, the astronomer (later credited with discovering the periodical orbit of Halley's Comet). In 1698, Halley had commanded the *Paramour* on a South Atlantic expedition that, because of his ignorance of the sea, ended prematurely in mutiny, which the Admiralty upheld as justified. Now it was specified that only a naval officer with wide experience could lead an expedition, and the scientists aboard ship would have no other responsibilities besides their work. First Lord of the Admiralty expressed that he would "rather his right hand be cut off than see a civilian command a naval vessel." Besides, the king had something else in mind for this expedition, a second objective, known by only a few trusted advisors, meant to make the most of his investment.

Cook represented a compromise. He was a respected officer of the Royal Navy, but because he had never commanded a ship before, likely was not the Admiralty's first choice. He was also, if not a scientist, at least a scholar of science, who had shown his interest and aptitude in this sort of work with his report on the solar eclipse in 1766. Both the Crown and the Royal Society could be satisfied with him at the helm.

Palliser also played a role in Cook's selection. Having ceded governorship of Newfoundland to John Byron, Palliser had recently returned to London, and soon would be appointed Comptroller of the Royal Navy. So his high opinion of James Cook carried significant weight with the Admiralty. Summoned by the Admiralty, Cook was promoted to the rank of first lieutenant on May 25, 1768.

Five days earlier, Samuel Wallis had arrived in London, fresh from his circumnavigation of the world, and was telling everyone who would listen about the island paradise he had found in the South Pacific. It was a lush and mountainous oasis, he said, where explorers could rest and replenish with fresh water and bountiful sources of meat and vegetables, without fear of the natives, who were friendly. These effusive descriptions made Tahiti the logical choice for the South Pacific survey that Cook was to lead.

Cook's primary mission was to observe the transit of Venus from Tahiti. The second part of his mission was contained in sealed orders, which Cook could not open until after he had completed the astronomical phase of the expedition. He was fairly certain that he would be asked to perform some feat of exploration. The plan was secret to prevent it from somehow leaking to France or Spain, and thus sparking a race for discovery. As far as the French and Spanish knew, this was purely a scientific expedition, and King George wanted to keep it that way.

Now, the Admiralty and the Royal Society had to assemble a crew. Most of the ninety-four people chosen for this expedition were Navy men - seventy-three ordinary sailors and twelve officers.

Twenty-nine-year-old Lieutenant Zachary Hickes was second in command. He was from a district of London not far from Cook's home on Mile End Road. Hickes was a skilled seaman having risen quickly from midshipman to acting commander of the sloop HMS *Hornet*. Historian J. C. Beaglehole, in his book *The Life of Captain James Cook*, described Hickes as "an invaluable man, probably, on any expedition, but perhaps born to be a lieutenant."

Under Hickes, thirty-eight-year-old Third Lieutenant John Gore was a sixteen-year veteran of the Navy. Gore had just returned from the Pacific with Captain Wallis's *Dolphin* expedition, on which he had served as master's mate.

At least one other man transferred from the *Dolphin* to Cook's expedition. Charles Clerke by now had circumnavigated the world twice – once with Captain John Byron and once with Wallis. Twenty-five years old, Clerke was the son of a farmer like Cook. But while Cook had started his career at sea on a merchant vessel, Clerke joined the Navy at thirteen. Cook had advanced much quicker. On this expedition, Clerke was only master's mate, reporting to ship's master Robert Molyneux, who was three years younger and had a fondness for drink that later would cause problems for Cook.

The crew included nine scientists selected by the Royal Society. Astronomer Charles Green had served as an assistant to King George's Astronomer Royal, and prior to that had been on the staff of the Royal Greenwich Observatory. Notably, he had been part of a team to test a chronometer - designed by John Harrison as a method for accurately determining the longitude of a ship at sea - which would prove invaluable on Cook's later expeditions. (By this time, very few chronometers had been manufactured, so Cook's expedition was not supplied with one.) Green was to supervise two other astronomers. Also on the scientific team was noted Swedish botanist, Dr. Daniel Solander, who had emigrated to England in 1760 and recently had been employed cataloguing the natural history collections of the British Museum.

Almost as notable was who was not on board. Alexander Dalrymple, deeply resentful at having been passed over as commander, had rejected the offer to sail with Cook as his chief scientific observer. Imperiously he had stated that he would certainly observe the transit of Venus from wherever he happened to be, but that he would not go to the South Pacific unless he were given command.

Of all the Royal Society members, Joseph Banks would have the most impact on the expedition. At twenty-five, Banks was fifteen years younger than Cook and already a recognized botanist. He had inherited a large fortune, which made him independent and helped him satisfy his wide-ranging curiosity. He had sailed to Newfoundland and was eager now to explore the uncharted regions of the Southern Hemisphere. Like Dalrymple, Banks had hoped to command the scientific endeavor himself. When it became clear that was out of the question, he began plotting schemes by which he could outshine Cook or usurp his authority.

Just as Cook sought recognition as a professional mariner and explorer, Banks hoped to be lauded socially and academically. The success of the expedition was equally important to both men, but for different reasons. Despite the difference in their ages and temperaments, the two became friends, even as Banks constantly challenged Cook's command.

Banks traveled royally, with a retinue of scientific helpers, artists, and servants. He paid £10,000 – more than double the patronage of King George – for the privilege of bringing his entourage (two artists, a secretary, four servants, and two greyhound dogs). Cook had no choice but to agree, though space was tight on his ship and this entourage required building new cabins. (This problem would crop up again on Cook's second expedition, with more serious results.)

By this time, Cook had already purchased a vessel and had it fitted out precisely for his purpose. The *Endeavour* was thoroughly familiar to Cook; he had served his apprenticeship on a north-country collier just like it, and the ship had been built at Whitby. First launched four years before, it had started out hauling coal as the *Earl of Pembroke*.

When Cook went searching for his ship, it happened to be docked in the Thames River, a mile from his home.

The *Endeavour* was a roomy, deep-waisted vessel whose broad, flattened bow tapered toward a square stern. It was a strong ship, built to stand up to the punishing sea. The 366-ton *Endeavor* measured 105 feet from the figurehead to the tip of the stern. Cook once said of his ship: "In such a vessel an able sea officer will be more venturesome and better enabled to fulfill his instructions than he possibly can in one of any other sort or size." But with a maximum speed of eight knots, it would travel around the world at the pace of a brisk walk. Because of its size, it was commissioned as *His Majesty's Bark the Endeavor*, to distinguish it from the four-gun Royal Navy Cutter of the same name.

On May 27, 1768, two days after he had been promoted to the rank of lieutenant, Cook took charge of his ship. Refitting took place at the Royal Navy's Deptford Yard, under Cook's close supervision. He was determined not to be like the captains who discovered flaws in their ships only after they were far off shore when it was too late. This work involved caulking the ship's hull to protect against shipworm, as well as installing a third internal deck to hold the additional cabins for Banks and his group. It took three months and cost £2,294 – almost as much as the Admiralty had paid for the ship itself (£2,840).

Five smaller boats - a two-masted yawl, a longboat, pinnace, and two skiffs (all oar-propelled) - were attached to the ship for support. The *Endeavor* was also armed with ten four-pounder cannons and twelve swivel guns, which Cook hoped he would not need. Provisions expected to sustain the crew for eighteen months were stowed in the ship's hold, including livestock, pigs, poultry, and a milking goat.

On August 7, James Cook left his London home to review his completed ship. He said goodbye to his wife Elizabeth, and his children (sons James and Nathaniel and daughter Elizabeth). Elizabeth was pregnant with their fourth child, Joseph, who would be born three weeks later on the same day the *Endeavor* raised anchor but die only nineteen days after that. Cook would not see his family again for three years.

The crew arrived sporadically to claim their quarters on the ship. The petulant Joseph Banks showed up on August 16; he was hungover from a night of drinking, and when escorted to his cabin, complained that it was too small. In another poke at the commander's authority, Banks announced he would claim the great cabin, which Cook had designated for reading charts and composing his ship's log.

Another ten days was spent waiting for a good northwesterly wind to carry the expedition out to sea. Finally, on August 26, the breeze blew in, Cook ordered his crew to unfurl the sails, and the *Endeavour* set off from Plymouth.

The Voyage Begins

The expedition's first port of call was the island of Madeira, 400 miles from Africa's northwest coast. There, they picked up fresh water, and about 3,000 gallons of wine. Cook also distributed a large quantity of fresh onions among his men to prevent scurvy. We now know that scurvy is caused by a deficiency of Vitamin C from months spent at sea without fresh fruits and vegetables. In Cook's time, the disease was still a mystery. He and other captains were beginning to believe it had to do with the ship's diet.

Scurvy exhibited as ulcers, labored breathing, rictus of the limbs, and rotting teeth and gums, which caused its victims to expel a putrid odor. It also seemed to rot the mind and wreak havoc with the senses. Variously mistaken as asthma, leprosy, syphilis, dysentery, and madness, scurvy is believed to have killed as much as 80 percent of Ferdinand Magellan's crew in the Pacific. But, by good management and luck, James Cook eventually would be hailed as the conqueror of the great sea scourge.

Cook was expected to test the theory – proposed by Dr. David McBride and Sir John Pringle, surgeon general of the Army and later president of the Royal Society – that scurvy was caused by a lack of "fixed air" in the body. McBride and Pringle believed this could be prevented by drinking infusions of malt and wort, which when fermented would stimulate digestion and restore the missing gases. The expedition had been supplied with a large quantity of malt, and these explicit instructions on its use:

> The malt must be ground under the direction of the surgeon, and made into wort, fresh every day, in the following manner:
>
> 1. Take one quart of ground malt, and pour on it three quarts of boiling water. Stir them well, and let the mixture stand close covered up for three or four hours, after which strain off the liquor.
>
> 2. The wort, so prepared, is then to be boiled into a panada, with sea biscuit of dried fruits generally carried to sea.
>
> 3. The patient must make at least two meals a day of the said panada, and should drink a quart or more of the fresh infusion as it may agree with him, every twenty-four hours.
>
> 4. The surgeon is to keep an exact account of its effects.

Later, Cook's report would tout the effectiveness

of malt and wort as a remedy for scurvy. He also tested the preventative effects of beer and sauerkraut. But the most protection came from the fresh greens and fruits acquired at each stop and Cook's strict rules regarding the cleanliness of the ship. Surgeon's mate William Perry reported that "sour krout, mustard, vinegar, wheat, inspissated orange and lemon juices, saloup, portable soup, sugar, molasses, vegetables (at all times when they could be got) were, some in constant, others in occasional use." Cook also stopped the common sailors' practice of scraping fat from the ship's copper pans to mix with their flour; it turns out that oxidized copper compounds eliminate vitamin C from the body.

Leaving Madeira, the *Endeavour* continued south and crossed the Atlantic to Rio de Janeiro, where Cook again intended to replenish his supply of food and water. Though the cargo hold was still mostly full, this was the last anticipated stop before Tahiti, and Cook did not want to take any chances.

Unfortunately, the Portuguese governor there did not believe that the *Endeavour* was a naval vessel, and was convinced that Cook and the crew were involved in smuggling. "He [the governor] certainly did not believe a word about our being bound to the southwest to observe the Transit of Venus," Cook wrote, "but looked upon it only as an invented story to cover some other design we must be upon...."

Cook and the ship's surgeon were the only men allowed ashore to bargain for provisions, and then only under the eyes of an armed guard. But, obstinately, Banks snuck ashore on a rowboat in the cover of night, with the naturalist Solander, to collect plant samples. He was determined to collect samples from as many countries as possible. One of Banks's artists, Sydney Parkinson, made twenty-two drawings of Brazilian fishes; and Cook drew a plan of the harbor.

They spent three weeks anchored off Rio de Janeiro, then Cook ordered the sails raised. But shots were fired as the *Endeavor* turned away from shore, the final insult from the Portuguese governor. Cook sent a crew ashore to resolve the problem, and after hours of heated debate, the governor finally allowed the British safe passage.

Despite this harassment, the expedition's first Christmas at sea was jolly. In what would become a holiday tradition, Cook doubled the crew's rations of rum, which loosened the men up to dance on deck and engage in playful fistfights.

By New Year's Day 1769, the *Endeavor* was pushing down the South American coast, hundreds of miles offshore to avoid any more trouble from annoyed locals. The ship sailed near enough to the shore of the Falkland Islands that Cook sighted penguins for the first time. Cook, keen to keep moving, ignored Banks's persistent pleas to land so he could get more plants.

The waters were calm and the sailing smooth until, some days later, the *Endeavor* entered the narrow Strait of Le Maire, between the eastern extremity of Argentina and the archipelago of Tierra del Fuego. There, a storm tossed the ship violently. Cook decided to backtrack and wait for calmer weather.

At Tierra del Fuego, some of the crew disembarked to look for wood and water. On the beach, as many as forty natives assembled to greet them. Fascinated, Cook observed and later described the natives in his journal.

These indigenous people, Cook noted, wore clothing made from sealskin, and streaked their copper bodies with red and black paint. They ate seal and shellfish, lived in huts covered with tall grasses and tree branches, and armed themselves with neatly made bows and arrows. But they did not appear to have any useful utensils, aside from baskets for scooping mussels out of the water. There was no chief or form of government as far as Cook could discern. "In a word," he wrote, "they are perhaps as Miserable a sett of People as are this day upon the Earth."

Cook was most intrigued by how casual these natives were about their European visitors. "They were so far from being afraid or surprised at our coming amongst them," he wrote, "that three of them came on board [the *Endeavor*] without the least hesitation." Some of the natives had buttons and cloth, seemingly of European origin, that led Cook to surmise that "they must sometimes travel to the Northward, as we know of no Ship that hath been in these parts for many years." They also seemed to be familiar with the European firearms, Cook noted, "making signs to us to fire at Seals or Birds that might come in the way."

Banks was less intrigued with the native people than he was the island's plant life. While the ship anchored in the icy Bay of Success, Banks and a scientific party, with some servants and seamen, climbed up the green hills that overlooked the water. The climb took longer than they had calculated, and before they could get down, they were caught in a bitter snowstorm. In the darkness, Banks forced them to keep going, well aware of the dangers of stopping to rest in the extreme cold.

Two servants failed to heed Banks's orders, and laid down in the snow and died during the night. In his ship's log, Cook wrote about this incident: ". . . these 2 men being intrusted with great part of the Liquor (that was for the whole party) had made too free with it, and Stupified themselves to that degree that they either could not or would not Travel, but laid themselves down in a place where there was not the least thing to Shelter them from the inclemency of the night."

The other men barely escaped death. Only Banks's unyielding spirit - and a vulture that he shot and cooked over a fire at breakfast time - kept them alive until they could return to the ship. Humbled by the ordeal and embarrassed that two men had died under his watch, Banks now gave up his plot to usurp Cook as commander.

Resuming the voyage, the *Endeavour* had a relatively easy passage around Cape Horn and entered Pacific waters for the first time. On January 30, 1769, the expedition reached latitude 60°10′, its "farthest south," and then followed a northwesterly course toward Tahiti.

Since leaving Cape Horn, Cook had been militant in enforcing the dietary rules he believed would prevent scurvy. He had collected berries and greens - the so-called "scurvy grass" - at Tierra del Fuego. And he made his men eat the sauerkraut he brought from England; it was brimming with vitamins, but bitter as brine - not the kind of food that hearty seamen enjoyed eating. In an entry in his journal, Cook detailed how he persuaded them to do so: "Men at first would not eat until I put into practice a method I never once knew to fail with seamen, and this was to have some of [the sauerkraut] dressed every day for the cabin table, and permitted all the officers without exception to make use of it and left it to the option of the men either to take as much as they pleased or none at all. But this practice was not continued above a week before I found it necessary to put everyone on board on an allowance [strict ration], for such are the tempers . . . of seamen in general that whatever you give them out of the common way, although it be ever so much for their good . . . you will hear nothing but murmurings against the man that first invented it; but the moment they see their superiors set a value upon it, it becomes the finest stuff in the world and the inventor an honest fellow."

Tensions rose on the ship as weeks passed with no land in sight. Then, on the morning of March 25, Cook saw seaweed – a clear sign that the ship was close to shore. But this hope came too late for a young Marine private named William Greenslade, who in despair had leapt from the ship to drown in the Pacific. Cook lamented in his log that "errors too great to be accounted for" had taken the *Endeavor* off course, causing the delays that had cost a man's life.

Finally, on April 4, an island came into view; it was Vahitahi, one of the nearly eighty atolls of Tuamoto, about 500 miles east of Tahiti. Sailing near the shore, Cook and his men saw many natives, armed with twelve-foot spears, and resisted the urge to land. Over the next subsequent days, the expedition passed through the Tuamoto chain of islands. Climbing the main mast to survey this tropical kingdom, Cook noted an island whose shape reminded him of a longbow; he called it Bow Island, a name it retains today. He named other islands in this chain for their shape (including Thrum Cap, which the natives called Akiaki) and discerning features (Bird Island, or Reitoru as it is known today, which seemed to be inhabited only by birds).

Tahiti

On April 13, 1769, the *Endeavour* anchored in Matavai Bay on the north side of Tahiti. Cook found Captain Wallis's enthusiasm was justified: The island seemed every bit as idyllic as Wallis had described.

Wallis had reported that metal of any kind was precious to the Tahitians because they had none, and that even a common nail would win their favor. Immediately after the *Endeavour* anchored, Cook issued a set of regulations to his crew. He stated first that he wished "by every fair means to cultivate a friendship with the natives and to treat them with all imaginable humanity." He insisted that "no sort of iron or anything that is made of iron, or any sort of cloth or other useful or necessary articles are to be given in exchange for anything but provisions." Lieutenant Gore and Master's Mate Clerke, who had sailed with Samuel Wallis on the *Dolphin*, had tempted the rest of the men with stories of trading nails to the native girls for sex. Cook made it clear that he had not come to Tahiti to exploit the natives.

Soon after the crew secured the ship, Cook and Banks went ashore, along with officers who had visited the island two years earlier with Wallis. Cook was relieved to find that the Tahitians were as friendly and cheerful as Wallis had reported. When the natives recognized familiar faces among the new arrivals, they called out "taio, taio" ("friend, friend") and overwhelmed the Englishmen with gifts of fruit and flowers, pigs and fowl.

The Tahitians were a beautiful brown-skinned people who spent their days swimming and fishing under the balmy skies. They were a hardy people - equally adept at wrestling as at swimming and dancing. They dressed in clothing made from the hammered-out bark of trees and wore flowers in their hair. Women as well as men were tattooed with geometrical designs, the result of a painful operation done with a sharpened bone covered with a sooty liquid.

The natives were clean, cordial, and hospitable, but Cook wrote in his journal that they "would steal but everything that came in their way and that with such dexterity as would shame the most noted pickpockets in Europe." Dr. Solander lost his opera glasses on his first day ashore, and the ship's surgeon lost his snuffbox. Once, after a feast, Cook spent the night ashore and his stockings were stolen from under his pillow.

When a brazen thief snatched a musket from one of Cook's sentries, another guard fired on him and killed him. Though this was a highly provocative act, the Tahitians seemed satisfied that the culprit had deserved punishment, and they remained friendly. One of the chiefs, whom Cook called Lycurgus, tried to compensate for the thefts by offering the Englishmen all of his personal belongings. When Cook refused, saying he only wanted the stolen items returned, the chief sent his people to retrieve them.

The most serious loss was the theft of the expedition's quadrant, the instrument the officers used to compute the *Endeavour*'s position. Banks, breathless with rage, hiked some four miles inland to retrieve the valuable object. But the natives, eager to possess every metal article they could find, had taken it apart. Banks managed to put it back together, but it never worked properly again.

Despite these problems, Cook realized the importance of establishing good relations with the natives. For one, he needed their cooperation to construct his observatory and the fort to protect it. This project required him to clear rocks and trees, which the Tahitians considered treasured property. The Europeans traded hatchets, linens, and other goods to the natives for hogs, bread, and coconuts. Meanwhile, Cook learned the language and customs of the Tahitians. When one of Banks's artists, Alexander Buchan, had an epileptic seizure and died, Cook ordered his body to be taken aboard the *Endeavor* and buried at sea, rather than offend the Tahitians by digging a grave.

Within two weeks of arriving on the island, Cook staked out a place on the beach for his observatory, which he called Point Venus, and eventually got the chiefs' permission to begin his work.

On June 3, Cook observed the transit of Venus and carefully recorded the calculations. The astronomical event lasted six hours, twenty-one minutes, and fifty seconds - on a day when temperatures reached 119 degrees, making the metal telescope hot to the touch. "This day proved as favourable to our purpose as we could wish," the commander wrote in his ship's log. "Not a cloud was to be seen the whole day, and the Air was perfectly Clear, so that we had every advantage we could desire . . . ."

Unfortunately, the results proved useless. Venus, perpetually shrouded by a cloud zone, cannot be used for accurate observational purposes. "We very distinctly saw an Atmosphere or Dusky shade round the body of the planet," Cook wrote, "which very much disturbed the times of the Contact . . . ." He did not realize it, but his observation was no more successful than those of scientists in other parts of the world.

Successful or not, Cook had followed his orders.

With the first phase of his expedition over, Cook opened the sealed envelope and read the instructions that spelled out his destiny.

3
SECRET ORDERS

"You are to proceed to the southward...until you arrive in the latitude of 40°, unless you sooner fall in with [the southern continent] . . ." Captain James Cook's sealed instructions also specified that if he did not reach land by latitude 40°, he was to go westward to New Zealand and find out if it was part of a larger land mass, the unknown southern continent.

New Zealand was discovered, but only partly explored, by the Dutch mariner Abel Janszoon Tasman in 1642. His expedition was the first to sail south of Australia, ending the speculation that Australia might be connected to the long-sought continent. However, Tasman had only mapped its western shore; no one knew New Zealand's geographical boundaries. The geographer Alexander Dalrymple was certain New Zealand was a peninsula that extended north from the mysterious continent. Cook's job now was to prove or disprove this theory.

Cook's secret instructions were hardly a surprise to him; he would have been more surprised if his mission had ended in Tahiti. Before fulfilling this phase of the expedition, Cook decided to have the *Endeavour* "careened." The ship was run ashore and tilted by means of ropes and winches to allow the bottom of the hull to be scraped clean of any plant or sea life that clung to it. Cook was happy to see that his ship had suffered no damage; only a coat of pitch was needed to seal the wood surfaces against leaks.

The *Endeavour* left Tahiti after a three-month stay. During the five weeks since the transit of Venus, Cook had charted and drawn sketches of the Tahitian shoreline. Meanwhile, the men had rested up for another sea voyage. They set sail again on July 14, 1769, and over the next month, explored the neighboring islands.

A man named Tupaia, one of the island's principal priests, left with them. He had learned some English and was eager to travel. Cook believed Tupaia would prove useful as an interpreter when the expedition visited the nearby islands. Cook named these the Society Islands, noting that they "lay contiguous to one another." As he hoped, Tupaia's presence put the natives there at ease. After a peace ceremony, in which gifts were exchanged, the Europeans had free reign over the islands. Cook noted that these natives looked and behaved like the Tahitians and observed some of their same customs.

On August 9, nearly a full year after he had sailed from London, Cook set his course south, and the *Endeavour* nosed into uncharted waters. Everything that came into view now would be new; everything would require description and interpretation.

Cook pressed on for nearly a month through choppy seas and high winds that damaged the *Endeavour*'s sails and rigging, but no continent appeared. A heavy swell from the south convinced Cook that the southern continent, if it existed at all, did not extend into the temperate latitudes in that part of the Pacific. "I did intend to have stood to the Southward," he wrote, "if the winds had been moderate. But we had no prospect of meeting land, and the weather was so very tempestuous I laid aside this design."

When Cook reached latitude 40° 20', which was slightly beyond the southern limit prescribed by his instructions, he turned west toward New Zealand, whose eastern shores had never been seen.

Late in September, after following a zigzag course - first northwest and then southwest - Cook saw seaweed floating around his ship. He knew land could not be far. At 2:00 in the afternoon of October 7, 1769, Nicholas Young, the boy at the masthead, shouted, "Land ahead!" He thus won the gallon of rum offered to the first crew member to sight land. The ship was just off New Zealand's North Island - a point on the east coast that was later named Young Nick's Head.

Cook's men soon discovered that the inhospitable coastline did not offer many suitable harbors. Sailing just offshore, they saw fires, huts, and canoes in the bay. "The land on the Sea Cost is high," Cook wrote, "with Steep Cliffs; and back inland are very high Mountains. The face of the Country is of a hilly surface, and appears to be cloathed with wood and Verdure [vegetation]."

When the Europeans landed, they found that the native Maoris were not friendly. Although the people understood Tupaia as he spoke to them, they were nothing like the amiable Tahitians. The Maoris frequently paddled out to inspect the *Endeavour*. Sometimes they would trade, always driving a hard bargain. But sometimes, without provocation, they would toss stones and darts at the startled crew.

Firing over their heads did not make the natives less quarrelsome or more obliging, as Cook learned one day when he ordered his men to discharge their muskets. The Maoris reacted violently, and the Englishmen had to kill one of them "upon the Spot just as he was going to dart his spear at the Boat."

The Maoris regarded Cook and his men with suspicion and hostility. The simple gifts that delighted the Tahitians held no fascination for the New Zealanders. They only wanted weapons of war.

Cook and his men often encountered natives on their scouting missions, and despite trying to gain their friendship, ended up killing some of them. In Hawkes Bay, they traded some bits of cloth for fish, but the Maori fishermen returned to abduct an Indian servant boy who had accompanied their Tahitian guide Tupaia. "This obliged us to fire upon them," Cook wrote, "which gave the Boy an opportunity to jump overboard. . . . Two or 3 [Maoris] paid for this daring attempt with the loss of their lives, and many more would have suffer'd had it not been for fear of killing the boy. This affair occasioned my giving this point of land the name of Cape Kidnapper."

Cook soon discovered that the Maoris were worse than thieves and kidnappers, they were cannibals, who ate the flesh of their vanquished enemies. The Englishmen recoiled at the sight of human limbs filling the stoves in the native villages and picked-clean bones strewn about. "I got from one of [the natives] the bone of the Fore arm of a Man or Woman which was quite fresh, and the flesh had been but lately picked off, which they told us they had eat," Cook wrote. "They gave us to understand that but a few days before they had taken, Kill'd and Eat a Boats Crew of their Enemies or strangers, for I believe they look upon all strangers as Enemies." Cook and his men feared they might become the natives' next great feast.

Cook made considerable progress in exploration in spite of the Maoris. Over the next six months, he charted the entire coastline. He cruised northward and rounded New Zealand's uppermost tip, then sailed down the west coast until he reached a thirty-mile inlet that he named Queen Charlotte Sound. In a beautiful little bay Cook called Ship Cove, he and his crew spent a month cleaning the *Endeavour* again. Here, there were none of the "mountains upon mountains" that they had encountered elsewhere. Instead, dozens of natural harbors lined the shore, strewn with smooth stones; and the rolling, green hills farther inland tapered gracefully down to forests filled with trees tall enough to be used in building ships' masts.

While the *Endeavour* was being worked on, the officers explored the surrounding country, poking through woodlands and cutting through thickets. On January 23, 1770, Cook and a sailor climbed a hill to see what lay beyond the inlet where their ship was anchored. Peering eastward, they realized that Queen Charlotte Sound opened into a strait that separated two bodies of land.

This strait was given Cook's name; his discovery proved that at least one part of New Zealand was an island, and a friendly Maori convinced him that the other part was also an island. "I had now seen enough of this passage to Convince me that there was the Greatest probability in the World of its running into the Eastern Sea," Cook wrote. When the *Endeavour* was ready to sail, Cook went through the strait back to the east coast and set out to circumnavigate this southern island.

The natives in these parts were more receptive, and when questioned, insisted that they had never been visited before by anyone like the Englishmen. Cook realized that wherever they went, they were first; and everywhere they landed, the men began leaving markers – "a parcel of loose stones, of which we built a Pyramid, and left in it some [musket] balls, small Shott, beads, and whatever we had about us that was likely to stand the test of Time."

Many of his officers still believed New Zealand to be an appendage of the elusive southern continent. But by mid-March, when the *Endeavour* had negotiated the storm-tossed waters at the southern tip of New Zealand and made its way up the west coast, they changed their minds. Even Banks, a staunch supporter of Dalrymple's theory, conceded later that he had seen "the total destruction of our aerial fabric called continent." On March 24, Cook was back again in the strait that bore his name; his circumnavigation was complete. To prove his achievement, he charted New Zealand's two main islands.

Now, his work mostly done, Cook turned poetic in his observations of this new world. He described "a narrow ridge of Hills rising directly from the Sea, which are Cloathed with wood; close behind these hills lies the ridge of Mountains, which are of a Prodigious height, and appear to consist of nothing but barren rocks, covered in many places with large patches of Snow, which perhaps have lain there since the Creation. No country upon Earth can appear with a more rugged and barren Aspect than this doth; from the Sea for as far inland as the Eye can reach nothing is to be seen but the Summits of these rocky Mountains, which seem to lay so near one another as not to admit any Vallies between them."

The men of the *Endeavour* were growing homesick. With his charts in hand, Cook felt justified in returning home. Although he had not seen the unknown continent or disproved its existence, he decided to break off the search. He wrote in his journal: ". . . as to a southern continent, I do not believe any such thing exists unless in a high latitude [near the South Pole] . . ." The next day, March 31, he sailed out of New Zealand waters. He named the last visible bit of land Cape Farewell.

Homeward

Cook's orders gave him the freedom to choose his own homeward route. If he sailed eastward, around Cape Horn, he might prove or disprove the existence of a southern continent; sailing west by way of the Cape of Good Hope would not give him the opportunity. But because the *Endeavour* was in no condition for a long, arduous cruise in the icy southern seas, Cook decided to sail west and stop in Australia. His plan was to scout Australia's uncharted east coast, then continue westward until he reached the colony of Batavia in Java. There he could refit the ship, if necessary, and replenish provisions for the voyage home.

The expedition made the most of moderate, westerly breezes, fair weather, and smooth seas to cover a great distance in the first few weeks. If not for a gale that blew the *Endeavour* north off its course, it might have missed Australia completely. By late April, Cook reached Australia's east coast, but harsh weather kept him from landing.

At dawn on April 19, 1770, Zachary Hicks, one of Cook's lieutenants, sighted a section of coastline that was eventually named Point Hicks after him. In contrast to the mountainous New Zealand, Cook noted, "what we have as yet seen of this land appears rather low, and not very hilly, the face of the Country green and Woody, but the Sea sore is all a white Sand." He saw the smoke of campfires in several places, certain signs that the land was inhabited.

Cook turned north, and on April 28, he found a sheltered bay in which to anchor. He called this inlet Sting Ray Harbor because it had an abundance of the large, flat fish whose barbed spines made them so fearsome. The shore of Sting Ray Harbor was rich with plant life that engrossed Banks and Solander so completely that Cook changed the name to Botany Bay, a name it still bears.

As the *Endeavour* worked its way into the harbor, the captain and crew spotted some natives spearing fish from a canoe. They paid little attention to the enormous vessel as it floated toward them with its towering spread of canvas. A few of the natives came onto the beach as Cook and Banks brought a landing party ashore. Try as they might, the white men were unable to communicate with these Australian aborigines, despite Tupaia's calls in his native Tahitian. The Australians wanted to be left alone.

The Englishmen, on the other hand, were fascinated by the dark-skinned natives whose bodies' were painted with broad, white streaks. The sailors were most interested in the natives' weapons, although they did not understand them; they thought at first that the boomerangs were curved wooden swords. They were careful to avoid the darts that the natives hurled at their boats, believing the prongs might be coated with poison. But on closer inspection, Cook realized the darts, made of fish bones, were "intended more for striking fish than offensive Weapons."

Fish in this bay were as abundant as the plants; dropping their nets into the water, Cook's men caught about 300 pounds of them in three or four hauls. Venturing inland, the naturalist Solander saw his first kangaroo, which he described as "something like a Rabbit." When they came upon huts, abandoned by the nervous natives, the Englishmen left gifts of cloth, looking glasses, combs, beads, and nails. But they were unable to forge any connection with the Aborigines. From his brief interactions, Cook concluded: "The Natives do not appear to be numerous, neither do they seem to live in large bodies, but dispers'd in small parties along by the Water side. Those I saw were about as tall as Europeans, of a very dark brown Colour, but not black, nor had they woolly, frizled hair, but black and lank like ours. No sort of Cloathing or Ornaments were ever seen by any of us upon any one of them, or in or about any of their Hutts; from which I conclude that they never wear any. Some that we saw had their faces and bodies painted with a sort of White Paint or Pigment . . . However, we could know but very little of their Customs . . . they had not so much as touch'd the things we had left in their Hutts on purpose for them to take away."

Disappointed, Cook left Botany Bay on May 7 and sailed along 1,000 miles of uncharted shore during the next five weeks. After he crossed the Tropic of Capricorn, on his way north, navigation through the coastal waters became more difficult - and then downright dangerous. The inshore waters were unnavigable because of shoals, and not far out to sea, the Great Barrier Reef presented a hazard Cook could not see.

This massive reef is the largest coral deposit in the world. The southern tip of the reef lies about 150 miles offshore, and runs northwestward for more than 1,200 miles, converging steadily toward the Australian east coast. Cook could not have known he was approaching a death trap, but he was aware that there were obstacles dotting his course. He urged his lookouts to remain vigilant. Because the ocean floor was uneven, he continually took soundings with the "lead line" to determine the ocean's depth.

On June 11, the sea floor became extremely irregular, alternating sharply between deep valleys and steep hills of coral. Toward evening, Cook appeared to have found an area of consistently deep water. With a smooth sea and a bright moon to light the way, Cook decided to sail on instead of anchoring for the night. Then he went below deck for a well-earned rest.

Just before 11:00 p.m., as the *Endeavour* was sailing along at the rate of one knot, the soundings showed a depth of about seventeen fathoms (more than 100 feet). Then, before another sounding could be made, the ship struck hard and remained stuck on a ledge of coral. This area would come to be known as Endeavour Reef because it nearly ended Cook's expedition. Banks described the ordeal: "Scarce we were warm in our beds when we were called up with the alarming news of the ship being fast ashore on a rock, which she in a few moments convinced us by beating very violently against the rocks. Our situation now became greatly alarming... we were little less than certain that we were upon sunken coral rocks, the most dreadful of all others on account of their sharp points and grinding quality, which cut through a ship's bottom almost immediately."

The crew had to act quickly to prevent disaster. Banks later told a friend that Cook "was upon deck in his drawers as the second blow was struck, and he gave his orders with his wonted coolness and precision." The *Endeavour* was thirty miles from land, and there were not enough boats to take all the crew to safety if they had to abandon ship. Banks was impressed by "the cool and steady conduct of the officers, who, during the whole time, never gave an order which did not show them to be perfectly composed and unmoved by the circumstances, however dreadful they might appear." As for the seamen, they "worked with surprising cheerfulness and alacrity; no grumbling or growling was to be heard throughout the ship, no, not even an oath..."

The crew followed the protocol for such emergencies at sea: They took in the sail and lowered boats to take soundings around the ship and to trace the edges of the reef. Anchors were lowered in the hope that the *Endeavor* might be hauled off the reef by pulling on the anchor cables. At the same time, the crew worked quickly to lighten the ship in every way possible. They shoved the spars used to hold the rigging overboard, and jettisoned fresh water, firewood, six irreplaceable guns, and forty or fifty tons of stone and iron ballast.

The *Endeavour* had struck the treacherous coral at high tide, and the lightening process took several hours. By the time the ship was ready to be hauled off the reef, the tide had fallen four feet and all the work was for naught. The men had to wait for the water to rise again.

Even with the high tide, and despite the loss of weight, the *Endeavour* wouldn't budge. But with the next high tide, the ship floated free, and was hauled clear and anchored in deep water. The crew then brought the *Endeavor* ashore to survey the damage.

A chunk of jagged coral had punctured the hull. The resulting leak was serious; the pumps could barely keep up with the water gushing into the ship. "Fathering" her worked better, a process that Cook described in his journal: "We mix oakum and wool together (but oakum alone would do) and chop it up small and then stick it loosely by handfuls all over the sail and throw over it sheeps' dung or other filth. . . . The sail thus prepared is hauled under the ship's bottom by ropes, and if the place of the leak is uncertain it must be hauled from one part of her bottom to another until the place is found where it takes effect; while the sail is under the ship, the oakum etc. is washed off and part of it carried along with the water into the leak and in part stops up the hole."

After the ship was patched, one pump alone could cope with the water, and the men at last could rest. Cook then found a narrow inlet deep enough for the ship to float close to shore and guided the *Endeavor* across a sand bar with only inches to spare.

The damage to the ship was nearly fatal; the coral had sliced cleanly through the bottom and cut away four planks. A piece of coral that had broken off and stuck in the gap helped considerably to lessen the leak.

The repairs took six weeks. At one point, Cook considered that it might be better to dismantle the *Endeavour* and construct a new ship from its remains. It was "in such a Shatter'd Condition," he wrote, "that we should be much better off if it was gone."

As the carpenters worked to patch the ship's hull, and the armory was busy making bolts and nails, the scientific team explored. Banks and Solander spent their time collecting botanical specimens, while others on the crew leisurely roamed, hiked, and hunted. They found little edible vegetation - a few palm cabbages and some pulpy fruit called plantains - but caught plenty of fish, turtles, and oysters along the shore.

Cook and his men were the first Englishmen to see such peculiarly Australian creatures as the kangaroo, the wallaby, and the dingo. They managed to avoid the more dangerous variety: pythons as immense as 300 pounds that could swallow a man whole, and crocodiles twenty feet long that lurked in the rivers.

During their time on shore, they tried again to communicate with the natives. But these natives turned out to be as aloof as their fellow tribesmen at Botany Bay. They refused the trinkets presented as peace offerings, and when they were not allowed to carry off turtles the English had captured, they lit a grass fire to try to burn down the explorers' tents and the linen hanging out to dry. The flames spread fast and far before Cook, firing his musket, chased off the Aborigines. Though one was shot, the natives were eventually convinced to lay down their weapons and go aboard the *Endeavour*. But they stayed only briefly; then, as they left, the natives again set fire to the woods surrounding the camp.

Cook described these Aborigines as "wholly naked, their Skins the Colour of Wood soot . . . their hair was black, lank, and cropt short, and neither wooly nor Frizled; nor did they want any of their Fore Teeth." None, he noted, were taller than five-and-a-half feet, "and all their Limbs proportionately small." They painted their bodies with streaks of red and white, pierced their noses with pieces of bone, and wore arm bracelets made of hair and cord hoops. "Their features were far from being disagreeable," Cook wrote. But efforts to understand them failed. Though "their Voices were soft and Tunable, and they could easily repeat any word after us," Cook wrote, "neither us nor Tupaia could understand one word they said." They could learn little more about these people.

Cook was eager to get back out to sea. The longer the ship was moored, the more depleted its provisions. The men did all they could to replenish the stores, but there were few good greens to be had. The best fresh meat came from turtles, which could only be found in abundance about five leagues out to sea, where the boats could rarely venture because of wind and weather. They hunted and killed a few kangaroo for meat, and stocked what fish they could. Luckily, they found fresh springs not far inland and were well-supplied with water. To boost morale among the men, Cook announced that "whatever refreshment we got that would bear division [would be] equally divided among the whole company." He described in his journal, "The meanest person on the ship had an equal share with myself or anyone on board, and this is the method every commander of a ship on such a voyage as this ought ever to observe."

In early August, when the *Endeavour* was ready to sail again, Cook sent his sailing master out in a pinnace to sound the depths, then climbed a hill to look out for patches of troubled sea. He hoped to steer clear of the Great Barrier Reef. "I saw that we were surrounded on every side with shoals," he wrote, "and no such thing as a passage to sea but through the winding, channels between them." Despite the repairs, the *Endeavour* was in poor shape; Cook noted that "many of our sails are now so bad that they will hardly stand the least puff of wind." Much care, he knew, had to be taken to avoid any risk to the ship.

Cook managed to steer the ship through the dangerous passage between the shoals, but before it could reach the open sea beyond the reef, the wind dropped. Now the danger was more acute; the ocean swells drove the *Endeavour* toward the reef. If the *Endeavor* struck the reef, the ship would be shattered.

Because of the water's unfathomable depth, no anchor could effectively hold the ship back, so the *Endeavor* drifted relentlessly onward. Later, in his report to the Admiralty, Cook gave this account:

> A little after 4 o'clock the roaring of the surf was plainly heard, and at daybreak

the Vast foaming breakers were too plainly to be seen not a mile from us, towards which we found the ship was carried by the Waves surprisingly fast. We had at this time not an air of Wind, and the depth of water was unfathomable, so that there was not a possibility of anchoring. . . .

The same sea that washed the side of the ship rose in a breaker prodigiously high the very next time it dies, so that between us and destruction was only a dismal Valley, the breadth of one wave, and even now no ground could be felt with 120 fathom.

When the ship was less than 100 yards from destruction, Cook sighted an opening in the reef, which he later called Providence Channel. His men in the boats managed to tow the *Endeavour* toward the gap, where it swiftly swept through. The crisis was over. In his report, Cook praised the men for their unflinching dedication: "In this Truly Terrible Situation not one man ceased to do his utmost, and that with as much Calmness as if no danger had been near."

Cook continued northward, determined to verify the existence of a navigable strait separating Australia from New Guinea, which Luis Vaez de Torres claimed to have discovered in the seventeenth century.

Some on the crew might have thought the commander was pressing his luck, but Cook decided that he would not allow himself to be judged as timid. It would be better, he reasoned, to die trying. "People will hardly admit of an excuse for a Man leaving a Coast unexplored he has once discovered," he wrote. "If dangers are his excuse, he is then charged with Timerousness and want of Perseverance, and at once pronounced to be the most unfit man in the world to be employ'd as a discoverer; if, on the other hand, he boldly encounters all the dangers and Obstacles he meets with, and is unfortunate enough not to succeed, he is then Charged with Temerity, and, perhaps, want of Conduct. The former of these Aspersions, I am confident, can never be laid to my Charge, and if I am fortunate to Surmount all the Dangers we meet with, the latter will never be brought in Question; altho' I must own that I have engaged more among the islands and Shoals upon this Coast than perhaps in prudence I ought to have done with a single Ship."

Working its way up the coast, the expedition reached the northern promontory of Australia, which Cook named Cape York, on August 21, and sighted the mouth of the channel between Australia and New Guinea. Torres's discovery could no longer be doubted.

Cook had achieved his objectives, and he was ready to return home. But first, he landed the *Endeavor* at what came to be called Possession Island, and in the fading light of a tropical sunset, took possession of the entire east coast of Australia. As the British flag was run up, Cook's men on the shore fired their muskets, a salute that was answered by those on the ship anchored nearby. The ceremony was one of thanksgiving as well as triumph.

Back at sea, the *Endeavor* sailed west, carefully navigating the channel that Cook named Endeavour Strait, which was south of the one Torres had found in 1606. On October 10, 1770, the expedition reached Batavia, where a month was spent overhauling the ship. During that time, many of the crew became ill, which delayed their departure until December 26.

Batavia was rife with malaria and dysentery, and though the men arrived there healthy, several died. Among the fatalities were Second Lieutenant Zachary Hicks, astronomer Charles Green, artist Sydney Parkinson, surgeon William Monkhouse, and the Tahitian guide Tupaia. Cook himself became ill, as did Banks, who arranged for a house in the country, where he quickly recovered, surrounded by fresh air and clean streams.

Only fifty-six of the ninety-four men remained when the *Endeavor* anchored in the English Channel on July 13, 1771, after a slow journey around the Cape of Good Hope. But none of the men had succumbed to scurvy.

Returning to his home on Mile End Road, Cook reunited with Elizabeth and mourned the deaths of two of their children - the infant Joseph and four-year-old Elizabeth, who had died just three months before Cook's return. That left two other boys, seven-year-old James and six-year-old Nathanial, who barely remembered their father. Home was not the happy harbor Cook had hoped for, and almost immediately, he felt the urge to wander.

In London, Captain Cook was hailed as a hero by the public, the Admiralty, and the king. He wrote proudly to his former mentor, John Walker of Whitby: "I had the honor of an hour's conference with the King the other day, who was pleased to express approbation of my conduct in terms which were exceedingly pleasing to me."

In his exhaustive report to the Admiralty, Cook suggested modestly that his discoveries were not great. But no other explorer had sailed as far, nor been as precise as he was in charting 5,000 miles of coastline. Cook was promoted to commander, and within weeks was at work on new plans. He had unlocked many secrets of the great South Sea but believed that a great many still remained.

4
RESOLUTION

After Captain Cook's triumphal return to England, there was no doubt that a second expedition to the South Pacific would be organized - and that Cook would lead it.

Others were as eager for further exploration as Cook: the botanist Joseph Banks; Hugh Palliser, Cook's early patron and now a man of influence on the Navy Board; and the geographer Alexander Dalrymple, who was still unconvinced that the existence of his "balancing" continent had been disproved.

Even Cook had backpedaled somewhat on his assertion that there was no habitable southern continent to discover. His expedition on the *Endeavour* had stopped thirty degrees' latitude short of the bottom of the world. Until he looked there, he could not be sure. He wrote to John Montagu, the Earl of Sandwich and First Lord of the Admiralty: "It appears that no Southern lands of great extent can extend to the Northward of 40° of Latitude, except about the Meridian of 140° West, every other part of the Southern Ocean have at different times been explored to the northward of the above parallel. Therefore to make new discoveries the Navigator must Traverse or Circumnavigate the Globe in a higher parallel than has hitherto been done, and this will be accomplished by an Easterly Course on account of the prevailing westerly winds in all high latitudes."

It did not take a lot to convince the Admiralty of the value of such an expedition. English pride had much to gain from another voyage. With rivals France and Spain redoubling their efforts to explore the Pacific, England sought to maintain its hard-won supremacy.

The Royal Society decided that Cook should sail with two ships instead of one, to increase the odds of success. With the *Endeavour* now on a routine voyage to the Falklands, two ships - newly constructed in Whitby - were purchased for Cook. The *Resolution*, the larger of the two, would serve as Cook's own ship for the rest of his life. It had a crew of 110 men, many of whom had sailed with Cook before. The *Adventure*, carrying eighty men, was to be commanded by Lieutenant Tobias Furneaux, who had sailed around the world with Captain Wallis.

The expedition got off to a rocky start, largely because of Joseph Banks. Banks already had sealed his reputation as England's premier botanist by publishing his extensive findings on the *Endeavour*. Many people in high society and scientific circles clamored to hear his stories of adventure on the South Sea, and newspapers heralded him. Another leading botanist, Carl Linnaeus, even suggested that Australia be renamed Banksia. The *Westminster Gazette* editorialized that "Banks should be the botanists' oracle, and they should raise a monument to him more lasting than all the pyramids."

It wasn't enough for the egotistical Banks. He wanted to lead his own expedition to the Pacific, and for a short time, believed that the *Resolution* and the *Adventure* were his to command. But then Cook, who in late 1771 had been busy charting the entire coast of England, had swooped in and taken charge. Disgruntled, Banks again set out to undermine the captain's authority.

Banks spent lavishly on preparations for the voyage and recruited a retinue of twelve men - scientists, draftsmen, servants, a portrait painter, even a pair of horn players - to accompany him. Just as before with the *Endeavour*, the *Resolution* did not have room for these extra passengers. To solve it, a new deck of apartments was built onto the ship.

But the new deck made the ship top-heavy. A navigator hired to test the ship's seaworthiness refused to sail it out of the harbor, fearing it would capsize. One of Cook's most reliable officers, Charles Clerke, told Banks: "By God, I'll go to sea in a grog-tub, if required, or in the *Resolution* as soon as you please, but must say I think her by far the most unsafe ship I ever saw or heard of." This opinion was shared by the Board of Admiralty and Cook, who insisted that the *Resolution* be restored to its former well-balanced state.

The *Resolution* returned to the fitting yard, where it was stripped of the new upper deck. Cook allowed only a single extravagance to remain: brass door hinges for his great cabin, which he paid for himself. Livid, Banks withdrew from Cook's expedition and went instead to Iceland. Cook wrote to Banks in early June: "Sir, since I am not to have your company on the *Resolution*, I most sincerely wish you success in all your exploring undertakings."

Cook regarded Banks's withdrawal as a minor irritation, but the absence of Daniel Solander, the naturalist, was a major loss. Solander had been one of Banks's cronies and did not rejoin the Cook expedition. Instead, the Admiralty sent two Germans, Johann Reinhold Forster and his son Georg. Each was skilled in natural science and botany. But though Georg was admired by everyone, his father was a peevish sort who proved tiresome early in the voyage.

Johann Forster, a descendant of Scottish lords, was promised a salary more than four times Cook's for the expedition and believed this entitled him to overrule the captain. Annoyed by this pomposity, Cook took to ignoring the elder Forster completely and encouraging his officers to do the same. When Forster would demand more time to gather specimens, Cook would refuse. Forster, in turn, threatened to report Cook's uncooperativeness to the king when they returned to England. (After his experiences with the Forsters, Cook would refuse to take scientists on his third voyage.)

Others from Banks's retinue left with him, including the famous German-born portrait artist John Zoffany. His substitute, William Hodges, was a landscape painter with a delightful sense of light and color, but a flawed perception of the "noble savage." His paintings of the South Sea Islanders were more romantic than realistic - and would further the myth, then popular in Europe, of the carefree savage living an idyllic existence.

Next to Cook, the most important members of the expedition were a pair of astronomers: William Wales aboard the *Resolution* and William Bayly aboard the *Adventure*. With an instrument called a chronometer, they would fulfill one of the expedition's major functions, improving and refining the means of determining longitude.

For centuries, mariners had known how to calculate latitude, their north-south position at sea. But since they never knew the exact time, they could not determine accurately how far east or west they were. The first marine timekeepers, controlled by pendulums, were fashioned in the late seventeenth century. But they were not particularly accurate because their mechanisms did not function well at sea, where temperatures changed rapidly.

Early in the eighteenth century, a carpenter named John Harrison had created the first reliable seagoing clock, which was spring-driven and remarkably accurate. Different metals were used to vary the spring tension so that, at any temperature, the clock could keep track of the time at zero degrees longitude. Knowing the time at zero degrees (site of the Royal Observatory at Greenwich, England), a navigator could use a sextant and astronomical tables to determine local time wherever he was. Then, by converting the difference between local time and Greenwich time from hours to degrees (one hour equals fifteen degrees longitude), the navigator could determine his ship's east-west position.

Though he was not recognized for his work until much later in life, Harrison's clock would revolutionize navigation and make long-distance sea travel much safer. He made four of these timepieces, the last of which was duplicated for Captain Cook. The size of a pocket watch, it proved a "never-failing guide" on Cook's second voyage.

The expedition was supplied with other advanced navigational tools, including a new azimuth compass designed by the English mathematician Henry Gregory. Cook personally requested this device, claiming earlier models had proven defective at sea "on [account] of their very quick Motion when the Ship is the least agitated." George's design added "some very engenious contrivance," Cook wrote to the Royal Society, "which in my opinion will in part, if not Wholy, remedy the defect."

Another apparatus aboard the *Resolution* would make it possible to distill fresh water from sea water. Both ships were armed - the *Adventure* with ten guns, and the *Resolution* with twelve six-pound cannons and twelve swivel guns - and outfitted with anchors designed to break through the arctic ice.

Finally, three months behind schedule, the ships headed to Plymouth harbor, to take on provisions for the three-year voyage. Cargo holds were filled with nearly 60,000 pounds of biscuit, more than 20,000 pounds of salt beef and pork, and 6,000 gallons of beer and wine. To prevent scurvy, Cook again ordered sauerkraut (nearly 20,000 pounds of it), as well as 140 liters of a marmalade made from carrots. Both ships also carried livestock - sheep, goats for milk, hogs, and poultry. Tools (such as knives and axes) and trinkets (beads, ribbons, medallions) were taken for trade with the natives.

In early July 1772, forty-three-year-old James Cook said goodbye to his wife and three sons; George had been born only weeks before, and would die at four months old, shortly after his father left. Already, tragedy had struck aboard the *Resolution* when, sailing from the Deptford fitting yard to Plymouth, a midshipman named Sandford had fallen overboard and drowned. "He was a young man of good parts and much esteem'd by the officers," Cook wrote after the incident. It seemed to be a bad omen for the coming voyage.

Fog and Ice

Cook's expedition sailed from Plymouth on July 13, 1772, with orders to round the tip of Africa and then circumnavigate the earth from west to east. Sailing the seas at the highest latitudes, he was expected to determine unequivocally the existence of a habitable southern continent.

The fame Cook had achieved with his first journey kept the second from being scuttled before it was really underway. Nine days out of England, on July 22, the *Resolution* and the *Adventure* were chased by two Spanish men-of-war off Cape Finisterre, on the western coast of Spain. The Spaniards opened fire and forced their way aboard the *Adventure*. Furneaux and his crew prepared to be taken prisoners. But after learning that the *Adventure* was sailing with the *Resolution* and the famous Captain Cook, the Spaniards allowed the ship to sail on. A midshipman named John Elliott, who at fourteen was the youngest member of the expedition, recalled the Spanish captain saying, "Oh, Cook is it?" and "[wishing] us all a good Voyage."

On August 1, the ships landed at Madeira to replenish their stores with fresh water, beef, fruit, and onions. Though they had sailed through several gales and turbulent waves, Cook wrote to the Admiralty to praise the remarkable qualities of the *Resolution*, which he said promised "to be a dry and very easy ship in the sea." The persnickety botanist Johann Forster, however, complained in his journal: "I had been seasick ever since the first day of our Voyage, could eat very little, was obliged to throw up my Victuals."

The ships stopped for more provisions at the Cape Verde Islands two weeks later and then reached Table Bay, just north of Africa's Cape of Good Hope, on October 30. The men on the *Resolution* were all healthy and lively, thanks to Cook's strict rules regarding diet and cleanliness. But on the *Adventure*, several men had already died from fever, and the rest were lethargic. Furneaux, the *Adventure*'s captain, paid little heed to Cook's rules, even after the commander gave him a stern lecture. Furneaux argued that the deaths had been caused by overexposure to the tropical rain, and from "bathing and making too free with the water in the heat of the day." But scurvy was the more likely culprit.

While anchored at Africa, Cook met the captain of a Dutch East India merchant ship, which in four months at sea had lost 150 men to scurvy; sixty more were ill. Learning this, Cook reaffirmed his orders regarding diet. Johann Forster noted that the men on the *Resolution* had already started to consume the second vat of sauerkraut, and "this time . . . liked it immediately & but few find faults with it."

At Cape Town, the expedition was joined by a Swedish naturalist named Anders Sparrman, who had come to Africa in early 1772 as a schoolteacher. Sparrman had met Johann and Georg Forster and agreed to come aboard the *Resolution* as their assistant. He wrote about this arrangement: "As the southern continent . . . had taken no small hold on my imagination, this was sufficient reason for me to congratulate these gentlemen on the trust reposed in them, and the good fortune they had in visiting as naturalists, so distant and unknown a part of our globe. I found them not only eager each for his own part to fulfill what the world expected and required of them, but they even went so far in their zeal for the more accurate investigation of nature, as to think of procuring an assistant, at no small cost to themselves, and therefore offered me my voyage gratis, with part of such natural curiosities as they might chance to collect, on condition of my assisting them with my poor abilities. Such an unexpected return to my compliment, had almost deprived me of the power of answering them, had my heart not dictated to me the most lively expressions of gratitude to them for the confidence they placed in me."

Since the ship was already full, Sparrman was allowed to sleep among the books in the great cabin. There was another change aboard the *Adventure* when Furneaux's second-in-command Joseph Shank became ill and quit the expedition. Twenty-one-year-old midshipman James Burney was promoted to second lieutenant; later recognized for his leadership, he would be made an admiral.

Cook's ships sailed from Africa on November 22, 1772. On the *Adventure*, James Burney spoke for most of the men when he wrote: "We lost Sight of the Land & now I look on the Voyage as begun & not before."

Over the next weeks, they searched for land in the South Atlantic that French explorer Jean-Baptiste Bouvet claimed to have seen in 1739, and believed to be a part of the mysterious continent. Failing to find it, Cook eventually decided that Bouvet must have mistaken an iceberg for land. Cook had little faith in French precision, but in this case, he wronged a predecessor. While Bouvet had not discovered part of a continent, he had spotted an island (later named Bouvet Island) that is nineteen square miles - 93 percent of which is covered by a glacier. Nearly 2,000 miles from the nearest land, this island is considered by many still today to be the "loneliest place in the world."

Temperatures plummeted as the two ships sailed farther south, and Cook noted "very thick foggy weather with snow." The captain issued the crew an additional supply of rum, along with "fearnought" jackets made of thick wool cloth to keep out the cold. Soon, they spotted huge glaciers, some as high as sixty feet and as much as two miles wide. "When one reflects on the danger this occasions," Cook wrote, "the mind is filled with horror, for was a ship to get against the weather side of one of these [ice] islands when the sea runs high, he would be dashed to pieces in a moment." Though the glaciers were a constant hazard, they provided a plentiful supply of fresh water when hacked into lumps of ice.

The cold and choppy South Sea wreaked havoc. "The people had not yet been prepared for such weather," wrote Johann Forster, "& therefore did the rolling of the Ship much damage, chairs, glasses, dishes, plates, cups, Saucers, bottles, etc. were broken: the Sea came in one or the other cabin & made all inside wet, or a lose box or cask stove out some bulkhead

& brought down a cabin. In short the whole Ship was a general scene of confusion & desolation." In the cargo hold, livestock acquired in Africa froze to death. Several men suffered colds, though Cook wrote, "they stand it tolerably well.... an additional glass of brandy every morning enables them to bear the cold without flinching."

Shortly before Christmas 1772, vast stretches of ice forced the ships to change course, first detouring west and then east in search of a clear passage. Cook gave Captain Furneaux a rendezvous location, Queen Charlotte Sound, New Zealand, in case the ships became separated.

On Christmas Day, Cook wrote in his journal, "mirth and good humor reigned throughout the whole ship." Considering the hazards of plunging full speed ahead with a shipload of inebriated sailors, Cook took the precaution of shortening sail. The crew of the *Adventure*, he added, "seemed to have kept Christmas Day with the same festivity, for in the evening they ranged alongside of us and gave us three cheers."

The expedition had sailed farther south than planned, beyond the temperate latitudes, where it was more likely to find habitable land. But Cook refused to break off his search. Explaining his compulsion to go farther, he wrote, "It is a general received opinion that ice is formed near land; if so, then there must be land in the neighborhood of this ice." The men spotted birds and penguins, which Cook believed to be further evidence that land could not be far off. On December 30, a midshipman on the *Resolution* named Bowles Mitchell wrote: "Pass'd an ice island which had 86 Pengwins upon it (I counted them)." Now, Cook wrote, the icebergs were "so familiar to us that they were generally pass'd unnoticed."

Keeping within sight of each other, the two ships crossed the Antarctic Circle in mid-January 1773 - the farthest south of any sailing expedition. "We . . . are undoubtedly the first and only Ship that ever cross'd that line," wrote Johann Forster, "a place where no Navigator ever penetrated, before the British nation, & where few or none will ever penetrate. For it is reserved to the free-Spirited sons of Britannia, to navigate the Ocean wherever it spreads its briny waves."

Though Cook couldn't have known it, the *Resolution* and the *Adventure* were only fifty miles off the coast of Antarctica, the sought-after southern continent. The ice became hazardous, and fearing his ships might be frozen in, Cook changed course. He ordered the ships to sail north and east, hoping to find an easier southern passage.

The ships stayed four miles apart through much of the northeasterly run, signaling to each other with gunfire whenever visibility was obscured by fog. Then, on February 9, Cook reported: "The thick foggy weather continuing, and being apprehensive that the *Adventure* was still on [the starboard] tack, we . . . made the signal and tacked, to which we heard no answer. We now continued to fire a gun every half-hour . . . the fog dissipated at times so to admit us to see two or three miles or more around us; we, however, could neither hear nor see anything of [the *Adventure*]."

Cook spent the next two days searching for the *Adventure* before deciding his best chance of reuniting the expedition was the New Zealand rendezvous he had planned with Furneaux.

He had to break through the pack ice first, which "surrounded [the *Resolution*] on every side," in huge blocks, "equally as dangerous as so many rocks," the captain wrote in his log. Cook hoped for daylight to make navigation easier, but when the fog finally lifted, his apprehension grew as mountains of ice, "which in the night would have passed unseen" came into view. "These obstacles, together with dark nights and the advanced season of the year," he wrote in his log, "discouraged me from carrying into execution a resolution I had taken of crossing the Antarctic Circle once more."

The men on the *Resolution* eagerly anticipated the warmer New Zealand climate; many groaned as Cook stubbornly plunged the ship south again and again, only to be blocked each time by the ice.

Morale sank as weeks passed with little in the way of encouragement.

But the South Sea was not without wonders. In late February, the astronomer William Wales recorded the phenomenon known as the *Aurora Australis* (Southern Lights): "The natural state of the heavens, except in the S.E. quarter, and for about 10° of altitude all round the horizon, was a whitish haze, through which stars of the third magnitude were just discernable. All round, the many streams of pale reddish light, that ascended towards the zenith."

Finally, on March 17, certain that no farther southern progress could be made, Cook sailed the *Resolution* northeast toward New Zealand. In his journal, Cook insisted that he meant only to rest and refresh his crew at New Zealand, before sailing south again to make another attempt to locate the fabled continent. "If the reader of this journal desires to know my reasons for taking the resolution just mentioned," he wrote, "I desire he will only consider that after cruising four months in these high latitudes it must be natural for me to wish to enjoy some short repose in a harbor where I can procure some refreshment for my people, of which they begin to stand in need of, to this point too great attention could not be paid as the voyage is but in its infancy."

On the way to New Zealand, Cook hoped to land at Tasmania to determine its true relation to the continent of Australia. But the wind was against him, so he abandoned that objective, too. He hoped that Furneaux, on the *Adventure*, might have had better luck with that particular mission.

Late in March, Cook landed at Dusky Sound, near the southwestern tip of New Zealand. One of his lieutenants, Richard Pickersgill, wrote: "We were regaled with the pleasing sight of the Mountains of New Zealand . . . how changed the scene! Everybody that was able to crawl on the masts and yards got up to satisfy their longing senses of a sight allmost forgot." Cook noted that, while he had sighted and named this bay on his previous voyage, he had never set foot here; "we were all strangers," he wrote.

They spent seven weeks overhauling the *Resolution*. The ship had been out of sight of land for 117 days, during which wind and ice had battered it severely. Meanwhile, the men explored the nearby forests, gathered fresh water from streams, and hunted seals for meat and fat, which was made into lamp oil. They met a few natives, including a friendly Maori family that, after peaceful overtures, went aboard the ship to dine with the sailors. Midshipman John Elliot wrote about Cook's ability to interact with the natives: "No man could be better calculated to gain the confidence of Savages than Capt. Cook. He was brave, uncommonly Cool, Humane, and Patient. He would land alone unarmed, or lay aside his Arms, and sit down when they threatened with theirs, throwing them Beads, Knives, and other little presents, then by degrees advancing nearer, till by patience and forbearance, he gained their friendship and an intercourse with them, which to people in our situation was of the utmost consequence."

The naturalists, father and son, and their assistant Anders Sparrman took advantage of the weeks on land to collect specimens and to make about seventy drawings of the native birds, fish, and plants. Astronomer William Wales observed the tides and used his tools, particularly the chronometer, to calculate their location by latitude and longitude. Cook conducted his own surveys and made his own drawings of the bay.

In mid-May, when the ship and men were ready to sail, the expedition proceeded north along New Zealand's west coast. At daybreak on May 18, the *Resolution* reached Queen Charlotte Sound, where the *Adventure* had been waiting for six weeks. Furneaux reported that, after the separation, he had visited Tasmania; and from his observations, Cook concluded - wrongly - that this land was part of the Australian continent.

Furneaux lacked not only thoroughness as an explorer, but also discipline. He had failed to enforce the dietary rules, and one man died while another twenty lay ill with scurvy. Cook himself went ashore to find wild celery and other vegetables for the sick men, and he lectured Furneaux on the necessity of herb juices, herb-tinctured beef broth, and preserved cabbages fermented with juniper berries. He also transferred one of his cooks from the *Resolution* to the *Adventure*.

Following the wishes of England's King George, Captain Cook also put ashore some sheep, goats, and pigs. The king, an enthusiastic farmer, hoped to populate the newly discovered islands with livestock. But the sheep soon died after nibbling leaves from a poisonous shrub, and the Maoris killed and ate the goats. The pigs survived and multiplied to such an extent that their descendants still exist in New Zealand, where they are known as Captain Cookers.

Before Cook arrived, Furneaux had planned to wait out the oncoming winter at Charlotte Sound. But Cook, who considered months of idleness bad for discipline, quickly dashed that plan. He ordered Furneaux, who had unloaded the *Adventure* to set up camp, to put everything back onboard.

There was no time to lose: Cook still hoped to traverse the entire Pacific, from New Zealand to Cape Horn, and end all doubts as to the existence of a continent extending into the temperate zones. Before they set out, the captains established two new rendezvous points - at Tahiti and New Zealand – in case they again became separated. Cook promised

Furneaux that if they did not see land after a few hundred miles, they would sail together to Tahiti.

Furneaux was not the only one to question Cook's plans. Johann Forster, a persistent nag, told Cook he was crazy to think he could sail south into the icy Pacific during winter. But, with the captain unconvinced, Forster and the others could only hope for the best. In his journal, marking a year since he had left his family in London, Forster wrote: "May providence continue to guard us against Misfortunes & Accidents, & procure me opportunities to describe & discover many useful things in these Seas & the Lands therein, for the benefit of mankind in general, & especially Great Britain & to the Satisfaction of the great & benevolent Monarch . . . & may I be enabled afterwards to pass the remainder of my Days in peace & retirement . . . ."

Threatened Every Moment

Through June and much of July, the ships sailed east and south through stormy seas. The weather was so foul that, on the *Resolution*, two men were hurled overboard, but luckily were rescued. Then on July 18, having reached longitude 133° west without seeing any land, Cook guided the expedition north toward Tahiti. He hadn't given up his search for the southern continent. He told only Furneaux of his intentions, before starting the homeward journey, to circumnavigate the globe at the high latitudes beneath Cape Horn, the southern tip of Africa.

To Cook, the detour to Tahiti was frustrating but necessary. Despite his orders, scurvy had continued to take its toll aboard the *Adventure*. Twenty men were ill and, ironically, the cook had died. The fresh greens were gone. The ships approached the south side of Tahiti early in the evening of August 14, but there they encountered another problem. Cook wrote in his ship's log: "I had given directions in what position the land was to be kept, but by some mistake it was not properly attended, for when I got up at break of day I found we were steering a wrong course and were not more than a half a league from the reef which guards the south end of the island. I immediately gave orders to haul off to the northward, and had the breeze of wind, which we now had, continued, we should have gone clear of everything, but the wind soon died away and at last flattened to a calm. We then hoisted out our boats, but even with their assistance the sloops could not be kept from nearing the reef."

With no wind, the ships continued to drift dangerously toward the reef, pulled by the inshore tide. Since they were in shallow water, Cook gave the order to drop the anchors; he could only hope they would hold. Luckily, the *Adventure* held firmly to the sea floor. But the *Resolution*, more than 100 tons heavier, sat too low and too near the reef, which battered the ship's stern each time the tide fell and "threatened us every moment with shipwreck," wrote Cook.

By heaving over other anchors and pulling hard on the cables, Cook's men were finally able to rescue the *Resolution* from the clutches of the tide. They were further helped by a gentle wind, which soon carried the ships closer to the island. Anchoring near shore, the ships were surrounded immediately by native canoes heaped with fruits and coconuts. Happily, Cook wrote: "The fruits we got here contributed greatly toward the recovery of the *Adventure*'s sick, many of whom were so weak when we put in as not to be able to get on deck without assistance were now so far recovered as to be able to walk about of themselves. They were put ashore under the care of the surgeon's mate every morning and taken aboard in the evening."

Cook soon discovered that much had changed on the island since his last visit.

They sailed to Matavai Bay, where many of the natives remembered Cook. The Tahitians told Cook of internal wars and that Spaniards and then the French had visited, bringing disease that had killed many on the island.

To escape the tide of Europeans, most of the natives

moved farther inland, leaving the villages along the coast depleted. The Tahitians there were angry and desperate, and immediately set out to steal all they could from the ships. Cook, disheartened by these changes, did not linger long. As a parting gift, one friendly chief who remembered Cook from before supplied the expedition with almost three dozen live hogs.

On September 2, 1773, the *Resolution* and the *Adventure* sailed westward to Huahine, another of the Society Islands. They stayed for two weeks, a mostly pleasant respite, despite some thieving by the natives. When they left, they took with them an islander named Omai, aboard the *Adventure*. Furneaux wanted to observe how a member of a primitive culture behaved in civilized England. Omai became the first South Sea Islander to visit England and return safely to his home.

The ships sailed next to the Tonga Islands, which Cook renamed the Friendly Islands, because the people were so hospitable and the landscape so beautiful. But still, he could not find the provisions, especially fresh greens, that his men needed. Reluctantly, on October 7, Cook gave the order to sail back to New Zealand for supplies.

Heavy squalls and a northwest gale made navigation difficult. Though Cook managed to keep the *Resolution* on course, he soon lost sight of the *Adventure*. He sailed back to Queen Charlotte

Sound and waited while provisions were loaded onto the *Resolution*. But after three weeks, there was still no sign of the *Adventure*.

Now it was late November; if Cook waited much longer, the southern summer would be over, and he would have no chance of crossing the Pacific again as planned. He left Furneaux a message sealed in a bottle, and buried beside the stump of a tree on which he carved, "Look underneath." Then he sailed southwest into the unmapped latitudes of the South Pacific.

By the time Cook reached latitude 66° south, ice and then dense fog completely surrounded his ship. Cook guided the *Resolution* northward until there was a break in the weather, then turned south to cross the Antarctic Circle, surpassing his previous record of "farthest south." Now the ship's frozen sails were as stiff as metal sheets, and the men on deck were encrusted with snow, as though wearing white armor. The temperature hovered at zero as the *Resolution* drifted slowly northward through the masses of pack ice.

On Christmas Day 1773, the men of the *Resolution* were far less exuberant than they had been a year before. They were healthy; there was not a trace of scurvy, and only a few had been felled by exposure to the weather. But it was hard to be cheerful when, in the freezing waters around the ship, as many as sixty icebergs came into view. "The whole scene looks like the wreck of a shattered world," wrote the botanist Johann Forster.

A month later, the *Resolution* crossed the Antarctic Circle again, this time attaining latitude 71° 10' - more than four degrees inside the circle, and farther south than Cook or anyone else had ever sailed. Cook recorded the achievement in the ship's log, but instead of being elated, he was discouraged: "I should not have hesitated one moment in declaring it as my opinion that the ice we now see extended in a solid body quite to the pole and that it is here (i.e., to the south of this parallel) where the many ice islands we find floating about in the sea are first formed and afterwards broke off by gales of wind and other causes . . . I will not say it was impossible anywhere to get in among this ice, but I will assert that the bare attempting of it would be a very dangerous enterprise and what I believe no man in my situation would have thought of."

Cook decided he would sail no farther in the South Pacific to look for the mysterious continent, believing that no European could ever hope to settle in such desolation. He turned his ship northward, but was reluctant to leave the Pacific because, "although I had proved there was no continent, there remained, nevertheless, room for very large islands . . . and many of those which were formerly discovered are but imperfectly explored."

On his northern retreat, Cook first reached Easter Island, which had been discovered by the Dutchman Jacob Roggeveen in 1722. Roggeveen had described the island as green and fertile, with tall trees and lush foliage. But now, fifty-two years later, Cook found it parched and dry, with trees no taller than ten feet. "No nation will ever contend for the honor of the discovery of Easter Island," Cook wrote, "as there is hardly an island in this sea which affords less refreshments and convenience for shipping than it does. Nature has hardly provided it with anything fit for man to eat or drink, and as the natives are but few and may be supposed to plant no more than sufficient for themselves, they cannot have much to spare to newcomers."

Cook found the natives friendly. They spoke and behaved much like the Tahitians, he reported, and were open to trade. Cook exchanged some medals "and other trifles" for potatoes, plantains, and sugar cane, which provided some needed variety to the crew's diet.

Exploring the island, the men saw the large stone monoliths that dotted the hillsides. Intrigued, Johann Forster wrote: "In what manner they contrived these structures is incomprehensible to me, for we saw no tools with them. . . . The Images represent Men to their waist, the Ears are large & they are about 15 foot high & above 5 foot wide; they are ill shaped & have a large solid bonnet on their head like some of the old Egyptian divinities. . . . These pillars intimate that the Natives were formerly a more powerful people, more numerous & better civilized."

From Easter Island, the expedition sailed on to the Marquesas Islands, which Spanish explorer Álvaro de Mendaña had discovered in 1595. After a brief stay, Cook and his men continued to Tahiti, which they reached again in late April 1774.

Off the coast, the Englishmen encountered an armada of native double canoes - more than 300 boats carrying 1,500 warriors in full war dress. As Cook described it: "The chief and all those on the fighting stages were dressed in their war habits – that is a vast quantity of cloth, turbans, breastplates and helmets. . . . their vessels were decorated with flags, streamers and other so that the whole made a grand and noble appearance such as was never before seen in this sea." He realized that his crew, nor any expedition of discovery, could survive if the natives rose up against them.

Cook learned that the fleet had been organized to assault Moorea, a nearby island that was at war with some of the Tahitian chiefs. The natives urged their English visitors to leave before the great battle began. Heeding this warning, Cook gave the order to sail west.

"No Man Will Ever Venture Farther"

In July, the expedition arrived in an island group that Cook named the New Hebrides. There, the people were black, rather fuzzy-haired, and as Cook soon learned, fierce. He recorded graphically what happened when he and two boatloads of men rowed from the *Resolution* toward a beach on one of the islands:

> Several people appeared on the shore and by signs invited us to go to them . . . When they saw I was determined to proceed to some other place, they ran along the shore, keeping always abreast of the boats, and at last directed us to a place, a sandy beach, where I could step, out of the boat without wetting a foot.
>
> I landed in the face of a great multitude with nothing but a green branch in my hand [which] I had got from one of them. I was received very courteously, and upon their pressing near the boat, retired upon my making signs to keep off. One man who seemed to be a chief . . . made them form a kind of semicircle round the bow of the boat and beat anyone who broke through this order . . . I was charmed with their behavior; the only thing which could give the least suspicion was the most of them being armed with clubs, darts, stones, and bows and arrows.

The chief then signaled for Cook to haul the boat up on shore. Instead, Cook stepped back into his boat, anxious to return to the *Resolution*. The natives seized his oars and brought the boat ashore. Cook tried to ward them off by waving his musket, but the natives were not fazed. Reluctantly, he ordered his men to fire. "The first discharge threw them into confusion," Cook wrote, "but another discharge was hardly sufficient to drive them off the beach." The natives responded with a volley of arrows, darts, and stones.

Friendship with these natives was obviously out of the question, so the *Resolution* sailed immediately for Tana, the southernmost island in the group. There, the natives seemed more hospitable, welcoming their visitors with gifts of coconuts. But that hospitality quickly ran out, and Cook's expedition was run off.

Cook sailed next to his New Zealand base, anchoring in Queen Charlotte Sound on October 18, 1774. He learned from the Maoris that the *Adventure* had been there and gone. The bottle that contained his message to Furneaux had been removed, but no message for Cook was left in its place.

Much later, Cook would learn that Furneaux and the *Adventure* had reached the rendezvous more than ten months earlier. Furneaux remained in Queen Charlotte Sound almost a month, but his stay ended most unpleasantly. Cannibals attacked, killed, and then ate eleven men who were gathering vegetables. A search party discovered evidence of the grisly feast: "Such a shocking scene of carnage and barbarity as can never be mentioned but with horror," said one of the men.

Steering homeward, Furneaux passed 400 miles south of Cape Horn and then crossed the South Atlantic, where he scoured the high latitudes, searching vainly for Bouvet Island. Finding nothing, he sailed to Cape Town, South Africa, where the *Adventure* was refitted for the last leg of its journey. The ship reached Portsmouth, England, on July 14, 1774 - a full year before Cook - making Furneaux the first English commander to circumnavigate the globe from west to east.

Furneaux was still recounting his exploits when James Cook reached Cape Horn in late December 1774, forty-one days after leaving New Zealand.

Cook's mission was almost completed: He had swept the South Pacific, and decided that "if I have failed in discovering a continent, it is because it does not exist in a navigable sea."

The crew of the *Resolution* spent their third Christmas in a miserable cove on the shores of Tierra del Fuego. Cook still had some bottles of Madeira, which he distributed along with "goose pie" made with local sea birds. The men rejoiced at the thought that, with luck, their next Christmas would be celebrated at home.

Early in January 1775, Cook sailed into the Atlantic and laid claim to South Georgia and an island group he later named after the Earl of Sandwich. Then he made one last sweep of the empty sea; though his homeward route passed within one degree latitude of the tiny Bouvet Island, Cook made no record of seeing it.

Continuing toward the tip of South Africa, outside Table Bay, the *Resolution* met up with a Dutch cargo ship of the East India Company. Cook went aboard and met its captain, who gave him some sorely needed supplies and told him of Furneaux's arrival in England some months before. At Cape Town, the crew spent a month repairing the rigging, which had been damaged severely by the South Atlantic ice. The ship was in good shape otherwise, which was astounding, considering that it had sailed more than 50,000 miles.

In late April, the *Resolution* headed north across the Atlantic, stopping briefly at the islands of St. Helena and Ascension, and finally the Azores. On July 29, 1775, the expedition sighted land near Plymouth, and a day later, anchored at Portsmouth, where Cook and some of his men took a coach to London. Their ocean voyage had lasted three years and eighteen days, the longest of its kind in history. Cook was further lauded for not losing a single man to scurvy, although four men died of other causes.

On two far-reaching surveys of the Pacific, Cook had discovered a host of new islands and, with the aid of James Harrison's chronometer, had charted the Central and South Pacific more accurately than anyone before him. He had proved that if the fabled southern continent existed, it could be found only in a desperately cold place. Summing up the results of his exploration, Cook stated, "I can be bold enough to say that no man will ever venture farther than I have done; and that the lands which may be to the south will never be explored."

5
POLYNESIAN ADVENTURERS

All of England celebrated James Cook's return - with a stirring reception befitting a man who had made the greatest ocean voyage in history.

Cook retired honorably from the Royal Navy with the rank of post captain, and as an added honor, was appointed captain of the Royal Hospital for Seamen at Greenwich. The Royal Society elected him a fellow and eventually awarded him the Copley Gold Medal, its highest honor. His portrait was painted by acclaimed English painter Nathaniel Dance, who portrayed Cook as a man of great natural dignity.

Other members of the Cook expedition received attention, but perhaps none more than Omai, the Society Islander who had been brought to England aboard the *Adventure*. London society and people of every rank were charmed by the native. And Omai was delighted by everyone he met - including King George III, of whom he said, "King Tosh, very good man."

Cook was surprised somewhat by the public's excitement over Omai, who had been in London a full year before the captain saw him again. When they were at Omai's home island of Huahine, Cook wrote, he had judged that Omai "was not a proper sample of the inhabitants of these happy lands, not having any advantage of birth or acquired rank; nor being eminent in shape, figure, or complexion." But Omai had proved him wrong, Cook wrote: "For . . . I much doubt whether any other of the natives would have given more general satisfaction by his behavior among us. Omai has most certainly a very good understanding, quick parts, and honest principles; he has a natural good behavior, which rendered him acceptable to the best company, and a proper degree of pride, which taught him to avoid the society of persons of inferior rank. He has passions of the same kind as other young men, but has judgment enough not to indulge them in an improper excess."

Omai was transformed considerably during his stay in England. He developed an urbane manner and wore fine clothes made especially for him. In contrast to the nobleman's façade was the Polynesian's brown skin, long hair, and blazing dark eyes. James Burney, who had been promoted to second lieutenant aboard the *Adventure*, served as Omai's interpreter, and the naturalist Joseph Banks, despite his exclusion from the expedition that brought back the native, paraded him in front of London's scientific community.

Londoners thought the native an amusing oddity, and enjoyed his wit and disarming naïveté. Many artists - including Sir Joshua Reynolds, founder and first president of London's Royal Academy of Arts - sketched and painted portraits of Omai, both formal and casual. Most of these renderings emphasized exotic features, such as hand tattoos, robes, and turbans.

Others taught Omai to play backgammon and chess, and in exchange, were regaled by his stories of life in the Pacific. Omai told them that when he was about ten years old, his island - Raiatea, the second largest of the Society Islands - had been invaded by a rival tribe from Borabora. His father had been killed, and Omai had fled with his family to Tahiti. Later, these stories would become the subject of a theatrical production, written and directed by John O'Keefe, performed at London's Theatre Royal.

Moreover, the British marveled at how much Omai seemed to know about the history of his island home, the islands nearby, and the whole South Sea Island civilization as well.

Cook knew that Omai was not uniquely well informed in this respect. On his first visit to the Society Islands, the explorer had noted that "these people have an extensive knowledge of the islands situated in these seas." And on his third voyage, recognizing that Hawaiians were of the same race as Tahitians, Cook would write: "How shall we account for this nation spreading itself so far over this vast ocean? We find them from New Zealand to the south, to [Hawaii] to the north, and from Easter Island to the Hebrides. . . . How much farther is not known, but we may safely conclude that they extend to the west beyond the Hebrides."

Generations of explorers who followed Cook were similarly puzzled by the native migration. We now know that, long before Spain's Vasco Núñez de Balboa first saw the mighty Pacific, native adventurers in canoes crafted from gouged-out tree trunks were sailing the ocean's breadth and colonizing its myriad islands.

These primitive people took hundreds of years to populate as many islands as James Cook visited on one three-year voyage. They guided their canoes by the sun and the stars, the wind, and their awareness of the shifting ocean currents - and have come to be recognized as perhaps the most skilled navigators, and most courageous sailors, of the ancient world.

Many anthropologists have agreed that the first Pacific voyagers came from various parts of Asia. These Stone Age peoples may have been pushed from their mainland homes by the arrival of other, stronger races - or perhaps were compelled by famine to seek new homelands. They migrated east and later south, along the Malay Peninsula. From there, it was a relatively short distance to Indonesia - the island group that includes Sumatra, Java, Borneo, and the Moluccas.

Living close to the sea, these former landsmen had to change their way of life. Over the course of many generations, they learned to fish, build boats, and sail. When they emigrated again, they ranged even farther - to New Guinea, Australia, and Tasmania. The distances seemed great, but the bays and straits were so dotted with islands that land was seldom far out of sight.

The islands in the western Pacific were settled sometime during the last few centuries before Christianity. But several hundred years passed before the uninhabited islands of the central Pacific were colonized. This region came to be called Polynesia (a word of Greek origin, meaning "many islands"). Shaped like the head of a spear pointing east, Polynesia extends from New Zealand in the south to Hawaii in the north, and to the apex of the triangle, Easter Island.

Many believe the settlement of Polynesia began in the fifth century, though the method by which the first inhabitants arrived is debatable. The most likely route of migration passed through an island chain called Micronesia ("little islands"), which includes the Caroline, Marshall, and Gilbert islands. But the precise path the natives followed may never be known.

Another mystery that may never be solved concerns the motive behind the push to the central Pacific. Did the Polynesians' ancestors fill their canoes with livestock and foodstuffs and set out deliberately to find new places to live? Or did their colonizing result from shipwrecks, or from boats being blown off course and running aground on foreign shores? Because of personal experience, Cook believed the latter was true.

When Cook later reached Atiu on his third voyage, he discovered four Tahitians living on the island. Omai, who was still traveling with Cook, was astonished, because Atiu was 600 miles from Tahiti. Omai learned that these four natives were the only survivors of a twenty-man canoeing expedition to Raiatea, about 100 miles west of Tahiti. A violent gale had blown them off course, and rough seas had capsized their boat. Starved and terrified, they had clung to the overturned craft for several days - until some natives on Atiu saw it on the surf and brought it ashore. Omai related the story to Captain Cook, who, fascinated, wrote in his journal: "This circumstance very well accounts for the manner the inhabited islands in the sea have been at first peopled; especially those which lay remote from any continent and from each other."

Gradually, calamity at sea became less of a factor in the Polynesians' movement, as they honed their shipbuilding skills. Observing some of the native shipbuilders, Cook was impressed by their proficiency. "When one considers the tools these people have to work with, one cannot help but admire their workmanship," he wrote. "With these ordinary tools that a European workman would expect to break [on] the first stroke, I have seen them work surprisingly fast." Their tools included "adzes and small hatchets made of hard stone, chisels or gouges made of human bones" - generally the bones of the forearm, though these were eventually replaced by spike nails from visiting ships. Most of the implements were attached to wooden handles by coconut fibers or sennit braids.

The native shipbuilders worked deftly, shaping the trunks of felled trees into long strips, which when joined became smooth, seaworthy hulls. When their tools became dull from constant use, the natives sharpened them on sandstone blocks. And when friction made the tools hot and brittle, they sank them briefly into the cool, juicy trunks of banana trees.

In many parts of the Pacific, the natives prayed to Tane, the god of the forest, for his consent before striking any tree with a hatchet. They also dedicated the canoe that was made from the tree to Tane, built an altar to him on board, and made daily offerings so that the god's wrath would not fall on those who sailed it.

The size of a canoe usually corresponded to the type of voyage on which it would be used. Larger boats were generally sixty or eighty feet long, but some are known to have reached 100 feet. These could carry sixty people, along with their pigs and dogs, and a supply of fresh vegetables - or 100 warriors, fully armed.

Slim, tapered, and expertly shaped to glide through the water, the native canoes could often reach twenty knots - a speed that astonished European sailors, whose ships normally traveled much slower. The natives used long paddles as rudders to steer the canoes, and smaller paddles to help propel them. They pieced together sails from cloth made of the dried, sword-like leaves of pandanus trees.

Many canoes were attached to an outrigger, which extended to the side to help balance the narrow boats and prevent them from capsizing. The larger canoes, built to carry supplies and people on long voyages, had a second canoe joined to them in place of the outrigger. On these "double canoes," some of which had as many as three wooden masts, the Polynesians' ancestors took their language, customs, culture, and traditions to the farthest Pacific Islands. And the plants and animals that were carried with them provided food for the generations that succeeded them in the new lands.

The pigs, dogs, and fowl found in Polynesia today came from the southeastern portion of the Asian continent. So did breadfruit, bananas, plantains, and coconuts. The sweet potato had a surprisingly different story; its origin has been traced, not to Asia, but South America.

At first, early Spanish explorers were credited with bringing the sweet potato to the Pacific; but later, scientists determined that this root vegetable had arrived in Polynesia even before Christopher Columbus discovered America. One theory holds that a host of South American Indians, set adrift in the Pacific on crudely fashioned rafts, were swept along by the ocean currents and southeasterly trade winds to an island in central Polynesia. (The possibility of such a voyage was confirmed in 1947 by Norwegian explorer Thor Heyerdahl, who, aboard a raft he called the Kon-Tiki, drifted 4,300 miles from the west coast of Peru to the heart of the South Pacific in 101 days.) But a more widely accepted explanation for the presence of sweet potatoes in the Pacific is that a native expedition (perhaps only one canoe) sailed from Polynesia to Peru, and then returned to its homeland.

This expedition must have embarked some 500 years before Omai left home on the *Adventure*. The voyage would have been long and hard, bucking the southeasterly trade winds, but with a push from an occasional westerly wind, could have been completed in three weeks. The land they discovered was forbidding, and the natives hostile, so the Polynesians probably did not stay long. When they finally made their way back home, they brought tales of the weary days at sea and of the strange, frightening land they had seen. They also carried tangible, permanent evidence of their transoceanic achievement: the mellow sweet potato.

Although the names of these courageous travelers are unknown, they were the first heroes of exploration in the Pacific. They crossed the mighty ocean and found its eastern limits, and they returned home to tell of it.

6
A NORTHERN PASSAGE

For several months after completing his second voyage to the Pacific, Captain James Cook remained bound to his desk. He finished editing his journal and attended to some of the duties required of his position at the Royal Hospital. He spent time at home with his wife and their two sons. Soon, Elizabeth was pregnant again, with another boy, Hugh, who was due in May. But Cook grew restless.

The public celebrations had ceased, and his own elation at having arrived home safely was fading. In a note to his old friend John Walker, he wrote: "My fate drives me from one extreme to another; a few months ago the whole Southern Hemisphere was hardly big enough for me, and now I am going to be confined to the limits of Greenwich Hospital, which are far too small for an active mind like mine. I must confess it is a fine retreat and pretty income, but whether I can bring myself to like ease and retirement, time will show."

He did not try very hard to learn to like his new life; instead, he wished for another adventure. At forty-seven years old, he was not too old for yet one more voyage, and soon, he got his wish. The final chapter of Cook's career at sea began at a February 1776 dinner in the home of the Earl of Sandwich, First Lord of the Admiralty.

That evening, the earl and Cook discussed England's renewed interest in finding a northern sea route from the Atlantic Ocean to the Pacific. If such a route existed, it would be a boon to trade. It would certainly be shorter than the course around the Cape of Good Hope, the southernmost tip of Africa, and probably less dangerous than the route around Cape Horn, the southernmost tip of South America.

England had been seeking this passage sporadically, and unsuccessfully, for 200 years. Early in the eighteenth century, Vitus Bering, a Danish navigator in the service of Russia, had discovered the channel (now called Bering Strait) that separates the Asian and North American continents. The English were so certain that this strait led to a passage over the top of the world that Parliament offered a prize of £20,000 (the equivalent of several million dollars today) to the first man who found that passage.

Cook felt it was his duty as well as his destiny to undertake the search. When the Admiralty offered him command of an expedition, he immediately accepted. Exuberantly, he wrote Walker: "I have quitted an easy retirement for an active, perhaps dangerous voyage. I embark on as fair a prospect as I can wish."

Cook was correct about the nature of the voyage, but he made a serious misjudgment when he chose to sail in the *Resolution* again. Although the ship had survived the extremes of tropical heat and Antarctic cold in the southern seas, it was not in good sailing condition and proved a liability. The expedition's second ship, the Whitby collier *Discovery,* was much smaller but easily outperformed the *Resolution.*

Part of the problem was that Cook, busy with the distractions of his retirement, for the first time did not oversee the refitting of his ship at the Deptford Yards. Because of this, repairs to the *Resolution*'s oak hull were sloppy, and seams were not tightly caulked – potentially fatal flaws which Cook wouldn't discover until he was at sea. Without Cook's overarching presence, the work at the yards dragged on, delaying the expedition's launch from April to July.

With Cook preoccupied, the expedition was fortunate to have other experienced men who thought of nothing else. Charles Clerke, who had sailed with Cook twice before, had been chosen as captain of the *Discovery*. This appointment was a consolation to Clerke, who had been led to believe that he was going to command the entire expedition. Having never served on a ship as higher than a lieutenant, Clerke gratefully accepted the chance to prove himself.

Cook's first lieutenant on the *Resolution* was John Gore, already one of the most experienced officers in the navy. Gore had been around the world with Wallis and had accompanied Cook on the first South Sea voyage.

Other members of the expedition included George Vancouver, a young midshipman who would later lead an expedition to the Pacific and make important discoveries along the North American coast; and sailing master William Bligh, who thirteen years later on the HMS *Bounty* would be overthrown in a famous mutiny. William Bayly, the astronomer aboard the *Adventure*, rejoined Cook, but the artist William Hodges did not; his place was taken by a Swiss painter named John Webber. There was a notable dearth of scientists on this expedition, which was how Cook wanted it after his bad experiences with both Joseph Banks and Johann Forster. Pressured to hire someone to collect botanical samples, Cook finally conceded to the choice of David Nelson, a young gardener who was given a crash course in botany from Banks.

Another addition to the crew was Omai, the native from the island of Huahine. Though Omai had been constantly amused by his London hosts, Cook noted, "His return to his native country was always in his thoughts.... He embarked with me in the *Resolution*, when she was fitted out for another voyage, loaded with presents from his several friends, and full of gratitude for the kind reception and treatment he had experienced among us."

Cook's ships also carried a large supply of vegetable seeds and some livestock that were to be presented, as gifts from King George, to the people of the Pacific Islands. There was a bull, two cows with their calves, and some pedigreed sheep. Cook remarked that the *Resolution* was like Noah's Ark, "... lacking only a few females of our own species."

Sailing Again

On July 12, 1776, Cook set sail from Plymouth aboard the *Resolution* – "weighed [anchor] and stood out of the Sound with a gentle breeze," he recorded in his journal.

But the *Discovery* was delayed when its captain, Charles Clerke, was detained over a financial dispute involving his brother. (John Clerke, the older of the two brothers, had sailed for the East Indies four years before with unpaid debts totaling $4,000. A court had decided to hold Charles liable, and prevent him from sailing until the debt was settled). Cook had waited as long as he could for Clerke; then, before sailing, he wrote a letter with detailed instructions.

The captains planned to rendezvous at Table Bay, at the tip of South Africa, the last civilized place Cook would see for a long time.

During the voyage south to the Cape of Good Hope, Cook's ship leaked badly, but he would not turn back. He made some repairs while awaiting the arrival of the *Discovery*, which finally sailed from Plymouth on August 1, nearly three weeks behind Cook.

The *Discovery* caught up to the *Resolution* on November 10 at Table Bay. Clerke told Cook that he would have arrived a week sooner if not for a gale that had blown his ship off course. During the storm, one of his men had been tossed overboard and drowned, but all the rest were healthy. Clerke had learned well from Cook, and unlike Tobias Furneaux, respected his rules regarding diet.

At the end of November, Cook and Clerke sailed southeastward together as planned. Their course would take them across the Indian Ocean; then, once in the Pacific, they planned to head north and carefully search the North American and Asian coasts for a channel leading east or west.

On Christmas 1776, the two ships were in the South Indian Ocean, anchored off a lonely spot that was eventually named Kerguelen Island after its discoverer, French explorer Yves-Joseph de Kerguelen. One of Cook's men discovered a glass bottle suspended by a wire between two rocks; corked and sealed, it contained a parchment inscribed with the name of France's King Louis XV and two dates, 1772 and 1773. Cook decided it must have been left by de Kerguelen upon his discovery of the island, and amended on a visit the subsequent year. But this marker did not stop Cook from planting his own, in an attempt to rewrite history. On the opposite side of the same parchment, he added a new inscription, naming this spot "Christmas Harbour" and claiming it for Britain. Then he put the parchment back in the bottle, resealed it, and placed it atop a small pyramid of stones on a hill. He also left a "Silver 2 penny piece," dated 1772.

At Christmas Harbour, the crews happily dined on penguins, other birds, and seal meat when their nets scooped up only about half a dozen small fish. They found a brook and replenished their water supply. They cut grass to feed the ships' cattle. But they stayed just four days. On his previous voyages, Cook normally took longer to explore and study a new harbor, when conditions and provisions allowed. Now, however, he seemed to be in a hurry - a man determined to leave his footprint everywhere, and running out of time. His journals from this voyage are correspondingly brief and rushed - offering little of the usual languid details.

The expedition sped eastward but soon was slowed by forces beyond Cook's control. First, the ships became enveloped in fog "so thick," wrote Lieutenant James Burney on the *Discovery*, "that frequently for many hours we have not been able to see twice the length of the Ship." As on Cook's previous voyage, the ships fired their cannons every hour to prevent separation. Then, a squall caused so much damage to the *Resolution*'s masts that they could not be wholly repaired until the expedition reached Tasmania in late January.

The ships landed at Tasmania's Adventure Bay, which Tobias Furneaux had named for his ship nearly four years earlier. Cook saw houses that resembled huge birds' nests made of sticks and tree bark. The natives lived on the coast, but they had no knowledge of fishing; they were content to scoop up mussels and other shellfish from the shallow inshore waters. A sailor on the *Discovery*, John Henry Martin, wrote about the natives: "They have few, or no wants, & seemed perfectly Happy, if one might judge from their behavior, for they frequently wou'd burst out, into the most immoderate fits of Laughter & when one Laughed every one followed his example Emediately."

It was a new island to Cook, but he chose not to stay to survey it. If he had, he might have altered his notion that Tasmania was connected to the Australian mainland.

In early February 1777, the ships sailed on to New Zealand and reached the familiar anchorage at Queen Charlotte Sound. The natives there feared that Cook had come back to avenge the eleven crewmembers on the *Adventure* who had been cannibalized. Few natives would board his ship until he made it clear that he had no plans to retaliate. Instead, when he learned the identity of the Maori man who had led the attack on Furneaux's crew, Cook sent an artist to paint the cannibal's portrait. "I should think no more of [the attack] as it was sometime since and done when I was not there," he wrote. "But if they ever made a second attempt of that kind they might rest assured feeling the weight of my resentment."

While the Maoris were relieved, Cook's men resented him for doing nothing to punish the cannibals. When they set sail again - after nearly two weeks spent restocking and repairing the ships – the crew on the *Resolution* rebelled by stealing extra rations of meat. Cook responded by reducing all rations by one-third, but then the men refused to eat at all, and he was forced to acquiesce.

Cook saw himself as king of the Pacific, with the purview to dole out mercy or wrath. He had shown the former to the cannibals at Tasmania; soon he would unleash the latter.

Sailing from New Zealand on a northeasterly course, Cook stopped at a group of islands that now bears his name. Then he swung west again to the Friendly Islands, a chain of 169 islands (thirty-six of which are inhabited) now known as the Kingdom of Tonga.

Off the coast of an island called Nomuka, the *Resolution* and the *Discovery* were greeted by canoes rowed by hundreds of natives, who swarmed the ships' decks. The Tongan women distracted the Europeans while their men stole everything they could. But soon, other natives - dispatched by a chief who recognized Cook as a friend – came aboard and began clubbing the thieves and hurling them into the sea. Witnessing this, Cook got the idea that he had been much too gentle with the natives who had caused him trouble.

Mostly, living up to the name Cook had given them, the people of the Friendly Islands treated him hospitably, but thievery continued to be a problem. Omai could not convince the people not to steal, nor were they deterred by threats that any captured thieves would be killed. However, Cook devised a means for recovering stolen articles: Native chieftains or other important men of a tribe were held as hostages until the missing items were brought back. This nearly always proved successful. But Cook had more brutal methods of making examples of the thieves.

By Cook's orders, thieves were tied to his ship's main mast and whipped dozens of times until their backs were bloody. In some cases, Cook ordered his own men whipped for dereliction of duty that allowed the theft to occur. When one chief stole a wrench, Cook had his arms bound tightly behind his back for hours until his people came to the beach with a hog as payment.

Some of the crew, who had wanted the Tasmanians punished for past misdeeds, now were ashamed by their captain's severity. William Anderson, the surgeon's mate on the *Resolution*, wrote: "I am far from thinking there was any injustice in punishing this man for the theft, as it cannot be determined what might be the consequence if such practices had been permitted. But that he should be confined in a painful posture for some hours after or a ransom demanded after proper punishment for the crime had been inflicted, I believe scarcely will be found consonant with the principles of justice or humanity upon the strictest scrutiny."

Other perpetrators got worse. When the whippings failed to reduce the incidents of theft, Cook tried humiliation and then mutilation. Thieves were released with half of their heads shaved - what

Cook called a "mark of infamy" - and later, minus an ear.

Cook believed that the natives respected, or at least feared, him. But they came to hate him, and then to plot his murder. Thirty years later, an Englishman named William Mariner, who lived on Tonga for four years, learned about this plot from the natives.

The Tongans planned to kill Cook and his men during a massive feast on May 19, 1777. The Europeans were lured off their ships with gifts of food and drink, and entertained with dancing and boxing matches. But when the signal was given to attack, nothing happened. Some of the Tongan chiefs had argued for waiting until dark to invade the ships, and killing Cook then; not getting their way, they abandoned the plot altogether. Cook never knew about it.

Because of contrary winds that prevented the expedition from sailing for Tahiti right away, Cook and his men stayed in the Friendly Islands until spring. The captain's cruelty toward the natives continued. Some of Cook's men were cutting wood for the ship when three natives started hurling stones at them. Cook had the Tongans captured and given as many as six dozen lashes with the whip. Then the crew watched in horror as Cook ordered a cross cut deep into the bicep of one of the natives – another "mark of infamy."

The Tongans must have been relieved when the English ships finally set sail on July 17. Three weeks later, Cook reached Tahiti, and the natives there got a taste of their old friend's new ferocity.

The two months spent at Tahiti were mostly pleasant and peaceful, but when a pair of goats vanished from the *Resolution*, Cook led a war party in search of the thief. He was so enraged, he admitted to his journal, that he intended "to shoot every soul I met with." Instead, he hauled away the culprit in chains, shaved his head, and cut off one of his ears before releasing him. But, since he was able to retrieve only one of the two stolen goats, Cook made an example of the entire village. He set fire to the huts and canoes. A midshipman on the *Resolution*, George Gilbert wrote about the natives: "all their tears and entreaties could not move Capt Cook to desist in the smallest degree from those cruel ravages, which he continued till the evening, when he joined the Boats, and returned onboard having burnt and destroyed about 12 houses and as many canoes."

The goat incident seems especially irrational because of Cook's mission to leave behind much of the livestock from his "Noah's Ark" to populate the island. Along with the goats, sheep, and pigs, Cook deposited Omai, who in little more than three years had seen more of the world than any Polynesian before him.

Omai astonished the other natives with his Western manners and extravagant behavior. He strutted about in European clothes, firing his pistols in the air and rashly handing out gifts. Cook, concerned that Omai might never settle down, decided not to leave the young native in Tahiti after all. Instead, Omai was taken back to Huahine, where he had come from. Even then, Omai pleaded with Cook to continue on the voyage. John Rickman, an officer aboard the *Discovery*, recorded: "Omai hung round the captain's neck in all the seeming agony of a child trying to melt the heart of a reluctant parent. He twined his arms around him till Captain Cook unable longer to contain himself, broke from him and retired to his cabin to indulge that natural sympathy which he could not resist, leaving Omai to dry up his tears and compose himself on the quarterdeck."

The ships' carpenters built Omai a house on Huahine, and others planted a garden. The Englishmen also left livestock for him to tend, as well as two natives taken from New Zealand to act as his servants. "I wanted to settle Omai in the best manner that I could," wrote Cook. But despite these earthly blessings, Omai died inexplicably within three years. Later, missionaries were quick to assert that Omai had been killed by "inglorious indolence"; perhaps he had been unable to readjust to his primitive culture after a brush with Western civilization.

The expedition was delayed for some time while repairs were made to the ships' damaged hulls, masts, and sails. Cook did not leave the Society Islands until December 8, 1777. Then, just before Christmas, he crossed the equator and sailed for the first time into the North Pacific.

Cook's old adventurous spirit was rekindled by the prospect of reaching blindly into the unknown. "Seventeen months had now elapsed since our departure from England," he told his journal. "With regard to the principal object of my instructions, our voyage was at this time only beginning, and therefore my attention to every circumstance that might contribute to our safety and success was now to be called forth anew."

North

The expedition's first landfall in the North Pacific was on an uninhabited, ring-shaped coral atoll - about ten miles long and fifteen miles wide. Cook reached it on Christmas Day 1777 and named it Christmas Island. (The first permanent settlers - fishermen and coconut plantation workers, who began to arrive in 1882 - called the island Kiritimati.) Carefully navigating the reef, the *Resolution* and the *Discovery* anchored there for a week, during which the crews feasted on fish, sea turtles as large as 100 pounds, and coconuts. Cook charted the small island, inscribed a piece of parchment with the date and name of England's

King George III, and left the marker sealed in a bottle. He also observed a solar eclipse before giving the order to raise anchor.

At dawn on January 18, 1778, Cook sighted land again - the western islands of Hawaii. He was the first European ever to see this group of islands, which he named the Sandwich Islands after the Earl of Sandwich, his patron.

Cook did not take time for extensive exploration, but he did observe the people. At first, he noted, they "thought they had a right to anything they could lay their hands upon, but this conduct they soon laid aside." When James Williamson, third lieutenant on the *Resolution*, led a party inland to search for fresh water, one native tried to pry his gun out of his hand. Williamson shot and killed the Hawaiian, and later was reprimanded by Cook.

The Hawaiians gradually came to trust Cook, as he did them. When some natives rowed out to his ships in canoes, Cook noted that "the only weapons they had were a few stones . . . and these they threw overboard when they found they were not really [necessary]." On the beach, observed midshipman George Gilbert, Cook was greeted by "a number of the Natives . . . [who] prostrated themselves before him in the most submissive manner imaginable." Later, after inviting several Hawaiians aboard the *Resolution*, the captain wrote: "In the course of my several voyages, I have never before met with the natives of any place so much astonished as these people were upon entering a ship. The wildness of their looks and gestures . . . strongly marking to us that they had never been visited by Europeans."

But Cook greatly underestimated the Hawaiians. He later would realize his mistake: that these were some of the fiercest warriors he had ever encountered, and they would not tolerate his abuses.

Cook's stay in Hawaii was mostly pleasurable. The natives eagerly traded hogs and potatoes for nails and pieces of iron, and "we again found ourselves in the land of plenty," Cook wrote, "just as the turtle we had taken on board at the last island was nearly expended." But the Englishmen could not remain long. An important mission lay ahead in northern waters. After about two weeks exploring the Hawaiian Islands, on February 2, the *Resolution* and the *Discovery* sailed northeastward toward the coast of America.

On March 7, 1778, Cook sighted the shores of North America at latitude 44° 30' (the Oregon coast). His two ships pushed slowly northward, staying close to land. But soon, problems with the *Resolution*'s masts and rigging forced Cook to land at a deep inlet in Vancouver Island, where he remained for most of April. Cook named this inlet King George's Sound, but today it is known by its native name, Nootka Sound. (The island would get its name from George Vancouver, a member of

Cook's crew, who was so impressed by its natural beauty that he led his own expedition in 1792 to explore the vast coastline.)

While repairs were being made to the *Resolution*, the men traded - mostly furs - with the Indians, whom Cook described in his journal: "Their face is rather broad and flat, with highish cheekbones and plump cheeks. Their mouth is little and round, the nose neither flat nor prominent; their eyes are black, little, and devoid of sparkling fire. But in general they have not a bad shape except in the legs, which in the most of them are crooked and may probably arise from their much sitting. Their complexion is swarthy... this seems not altogether natural but proceeds partly from smoke, dirt, and paint, for they paint with a liberal hand and are slovenly and dirty to the last degree."

Cook acknowledged that some of the Indians he saw had a certain dignity, but he said their houses were "as filthy as hogsties, everything in and about them stinking of fish, oil, and smoke."

After Vancouver Island, the expedition made swift progress up the west coast of Canada. Careful scrutiny was unnecessary, because the snowy, towering peaks of the coastal ranges suggested that no passage to the east would be found there.

In early May, the two ships landed at another inlet, after a heavy gale punched more leaks into the much-repaired hull of the *Resolution*. There, Cook had his first brush with the Eskimos, who greeted him with drawn knives. The Eskimos, eager to rob the expedition, did not recoil when they saw the English firearms but gave up when they realized that Cook's men had longer knives than they did. Cook boasted that his party "had the good fortune to leave [the Eskimos] as ignorant as we found them, for they neither heard nor saw a musket fired unless at birds."

As the ships sailed onward, the coast began to bend in a westerly direction. When Cook saw a break in the land, he was certain he had found at last the channel he had been searching for. His ships had sailed almost 100 miles into the opening before he realized that it was not a channel, but a sound (Prince William Sound). So the search continued.

On June 1, Cook's ships entered another deep inlet (Cook Inlet). He did not think this was the sought-after gateway to the northern passage, but he explored it to make sure. Before turning back, Cook reported, he sent two small boats ashore to "take possession of the country and river in His Majesty's name, and to bury in the ground a bottle containing two pieces of English coin (dated 1772) and a paper on which was inscribed the ships' names, date, etc."

By the end of June, the expedition had passed through the Aleutian Islands and had turned north to follow the Alaska shoreline once again. This part of the voyage was slow and difficult. Fog and wind proved troublesome to navigation, as did the ridges of rock that sometimes ran as far as twenty miles into the sea from the shore. Once, the *Resolution* smacked into a sandbank, and the *Discovery* barely avoided making the same mistake.

Heading north, Cook entered the Bering Strait, which already was becoming choked with ice. On August 9, 1778, he sighted the westernmost point of North America, which he named Cape Prince of Wales. The next day, his ships crossed the narrowest neck of the strait - only fifty-six miles wide - and landed on the eastern tip of Asia. He was almost as far north as the Arctic Circle. But with cold weather approaching, the farther he sailed, the more ice there was to hinder his passage. The best of the summer season had passed.

During the last days of August, Cook steered his ships back and forth - between Asia and America - looking for a break in the ice pack. Fog and heavy snowfall impaired visibility, making the search more difficult. Compounding the problem, ice clung to the ships' rigging, and the decks had to be continually cleared of snow.

When the ships reached latitude 70° 44' (nearly as far north as Cook had ever sailed south), the fog lifted momentarily to reveal a wall of ice ten or twelve feet high. This was the farthest north that Cook would reach – and, though he didn't know it, only about fifty miles from his goal, the entrance to the Northwest Passage. On August 29, realizing that further penetration was impossible, he decided to direct his ships back to Hawaii and resume his search the following summer. There was nothing more he could do. In his journal, Cook justified this move: "The season was not so far advanced and the time when the frost is expected to set in so near at hand, that I did not think it consistent with prudence to make any further attempts to find a passage this year in any direction, so little was the prospect of succeeding. My attention was now directed towards finding some place where we could obtain wood and water, and in considering how I should spend the winter, so as to make some improvement to geography and navigation and at the same time be in a condition to return to the North in further search of a passage the ensuing summer."

On the way south, Cook landed briefly at Unalaska Island, one of the Aleutians, so that more repairs could be made to the *Resolution*. The ship's sails were in poor condition, its rigging showed signs of wear, and a gale had done fresh damage to the hull. But, because of the approach of cold weather, most of the needed repairs could not be made until the expedition returned to the Hawaiian Islands. Unalaska provided all the fresh fish, water, and berries the men needed, but even their fearnought jackets were not heavy enough to protect them from a harsh arctic winter. "The ice was seen hanging at our hair, our noses, and even at the men's finger's ends," wrote John Rickman, second lieutenant on the *Discovery*, "if they did but expose them to the air for five or six minutes."

Emergency repairs had to be made at sea when a violent storm toppled the main mast on the *Discovery*. One man, Captain Clerke's servant aboard the *Discovery*, was crushed and killed, and four others were injured in the catastrophe. Some days later, a squall ripped the topsail on the *Resolution*. Luckily, the weather cleared as the battered ships made their way farther south.

"This Is Not Rono"

Hawaii was sighted again by late November. But for the next eight weeks, the ships fought off high winds and bad weather as Cook looked for a safe harbor, free from punishing gales. Briefly, while rounding Hawaii's eastern point, the ships became separated. They finally found Kealakekua Bay on the west side of Hawaii, the biggest island in the group, and landed on January 17, 1779. There, Cook was given the best reception of his life, though it would also be his last.

The ships came to rest as natives, on 800 canoes, rowed out from the shore and joyously surrounded them. When Cook at last gave the order to unbend the sails and strike the yards, he noted, "I have nowhere in this sea seen such a number of people assembled in one place. Besides those in the canoes, all the shore of the bay was covered with people, and hundreds were swimming about the ships like shoals of fish." This happy passage is the final entry in Cook's journal.

Neither Cook nor his men understood why they were welcomed back with such ceremony. They could not have known that the native priests had decided Cook was the Hawaiian god of the new year, Rono, who, according to legend, conferred peace and happiness on his subjects. Rono had sailed away from Hawaii many years earlier, the legend said, but before leaving he had prophesied that he would return one day in a great ship carrying a forest of small trees.

Cook had not one but two great ships whose masts looked like trees. He had come now for the second time in less than a year. Thus, the islanders assumed that their god had returned. They brought him gifts, and their chiefs had elaborate ceremonies staged in his honor. He was given a bright red cloak, and the island king, old Terreeoboo, placed a feathered helmet on Cook's head. David Samwell, the surgeon on the *Discovery*, described one such ceremony honoring the captain: "A Priest whose name is Coo-a-ha attended by others of the same order led Captn Cook to the top of a Pile of stones called O-he-kee-aw, which is a sacred place, & on which the images of their Gods are placed & two of three Houses & kind of altars all dedicated to religious Uses; on the poles with which this place is surrounded were stuck twenty human Skulls, of Men who had been offered as Sacrifices to their Gods. The Priest performed various Ceremonies on this Occasion, he killed a pig at Captn Cook's feet, at the same time chanting some words in concert with his Attendants, he then went round & touched the images one by one.... The priest took some of the fat which probably he looked upon as holy oil & anointed Captn Cook's Arms & other parts with it, the Priests at the same time chanting their Hymns or whatever they may be called."

During the ceremony, other crewmen noted, Cook "was quite passive," and content to let the priest do whatever he pleased. But Cook's enjoyment at being revered did not last. Soon the natives would treat him as a mortal - and then as a mortal enemy.

James King, second lieutenant on the *Discovery*, observed: "It is very clear ... [the natives] regard us as a set of beings infinitely their superiors; should this respect wear away from familiarity, or by length of intercourse, their behavior may change." And so it did.

Two weeks passed, and the enthusiasm of the natives began to subside. They had lavished their visitors with fruit, vegetables, coconuts, and pigs - all of which were consumed quickly. But the appetites of the hungry seamen threatened to exhaust the islanders' generosity. One of Cook's lieutenants noted how the natives began "stroking the sides and patting the bellies of the sailors . . . telling them partly by signs and partly by words that it was time for them to go."

Then, on February 1, the Hawaiians' suspicions - that their visitors were not gods, but mere men - were confirmed. That day, a gunner's mate named William Watman had a paralytic stroke and died. Watman was an old man, having sailed as a Marine for twenty-one years and twice with Cook. The natives watched as he was buried on the sacred ground usually reserved for their chiefs, in a ceremony performed by Cook and one of the Hawaiian priests. The next day, some chiefs asked Cook and his men when they might leave, and "seemd well pleased that it was to be soon," wrote Lieutenant King.

On February 4, aware of the natives' growing hostility, Cook gave the order to set sail. He hoped to find another good anchorage farther north, but once again, the *Resolution* proved troublesome. Struck by a new gale, the ship's sails were split, and the foremast was sprung. A week later, both ships returned to Kealakekua Bay.

This time, the reception was different. No canoes came out to meet them, and when Lieutenant James King led a party ashore, the islanders were unfriendly and resentful. As King rowed back to the *Resolution*, he saw a native canoe paddling away from the *Discovery*. He learned later that as Captain Clerke was entertaining a chief in his cabin, a thief had climbed up the side of the ship, run across the deck in full view, snatched the armorer's chisel and tongs, and jumped overboard into a waiting canoe.

The incident was reported at once to Cook, who sent a party - led by Thomas Edgar and midshipman George Vancouver - to recover the stolen tools and capture the thief. After some argument with the natives, Edgar succeeded in retrieving the tongs and chisel, but the thief had vanished. As a reprisal, Edgar seized a native canoe from the beach and got into a scuffle with the canoe's owner, a young chief named Parea.

Edgar struck the chief on the head with an oar, but Vancouver, who tried to intervene, was knocked down. A shower of stones then forced the Englishmen to swim out to a rock a short distance from shore, leaving their boat unguarded. The natives immediately swarmed into the boat, removing whatever articles they could find - even Vancouver's cap. They would have demolished the boat entirely if Parea had not recovered from his blow in time to drive them off. The Englishmen swam back to shore, and Parea, fearful that Rono might kill him for starting the disturbance, begged Edgar's forgiveness.

When Cook learned about the fight, he was furious, and blamed Edgar for mishandling the assignment. Now, the temper of the islanders clearly was rising. "I am afraid," Cook told his men, "that these people will oblige me to use some violent measures, for they must not be left to imagine they have gained an advantage over us." Someone suggested that there might be strong native resistance to any attempt at retribution, but Cook insisted, "They will not stand the fire of a single musket." He was certain that his men could suppress the populace just by firing a shot or two.

At daybreak the next morning, February 14, Cook learned that the *Discovery*'s cutter had been stolen overnight. The captain decided to follow a practice that had always been successful in cases of serious theft: to take an important hostage until the stolen item was returned. He armed his marines and loaded his double-barreled musket - one barrel with small shot to scatter a crowd, the other with ball to kill.

Cook and nine men, commanded by Lieutenant Molesworth Phillips, rowed ashore in two boats. A third boat was sent to the other side of the bay to prevent the natives from organizing a counterattack with their canoes. The climactic hour of Cook's career was at hand. Lieutenant Phillips, in his report to Captain Clerke, recorded everything that took place in that brief but crucial span of time.

As soon as Cook landed, he made his way to the village of King Terreeoboo. After a short talk, he realized that Terreeoboo knew nothing about the theft of the cutter. But Cook, planning to make Terreeoboo his hostage, invited him aboard the *Resolution* so they could continue their discussion. Terreeoboo agreed to go, but the crowd of natives that had gathered outside his hut protested loudly. They told the king that Cook would surely kill him, and they appeared determined to keep him from going.

Phillips ordered his men to make a lane through the crowd all the way to the beach. Cook and his hostage passed easily through the lane, but when they were in sight of the boats, a woman broke through the cordon and begged the king not to go. She was, it seemed, his favorite wife. As she threw her arms around her husband, the mob surged forward, pressing the Englishmen so close that they could not fire their muskets. Phillips sensed that the situation was becoming dangerous, and asked Cook if the men should be drawn up close to the water's edge to secure a retreat. Cook replied coolly that there was no real danger, but that Phillips could do as he wished. So the Englishmen formed a line along the shore, standing with their backs to the sea.

Cook stood some twenty-five yards away from the beach, trying to persuade the king to ignore his wife's entreaties and go aboard the *Resolution*. The old Hawaiian was sitting on the ground, looking frightened and dejected; every time he made a move to follow Cook, the chiefs stopped him. One of them tried to hit Cook in the face with a breadfruit. Another was about to hurl a stone when a fellow native restrained his arm.

Cook was ready to give up trying to take the king and order a withdrawal from the beach when a native runner burst through the crowd. The islander relayed the news that the English party on the other side of the bay had fired on a canoe and killed an important chief. This shocked the mob into action. The men began putting on their war cloaks, and many stooped to gather handfuls of stones. Others shook their clubs and spears fiercely.

Cook finally realized that the situation was as dangerous as Phillips had imagined it would be. He and Phillips started walking down to the water as the Hawaiians' shouts grew louder and angrier.

An islander came menacingly near, brandishing an iron spike and a sharp stone. Cook turned around in time to fire a charge of small shot, which made no impression on the assailant's thick cloak. He fired at the man again - this time discharging ball - and killed another islander instead. Retaliating, the natives began to march on the line of Englishmen, filling the air with a rain of stones.

The Englishmen fired a volley, which halted the rioters, but only for a moment. The natives continued to advance while the muskets were being reloaded - an operation that took several minutes. During the interval, Cook was seen making his way down to the beach, shouting to the boats to pull in closer. One boat came very near the rocks offshore, but was still several yards from the beach. It would have taken only a few minutes for Cook to wade out and be pulled aboard, but before he could, he was surrounded.

One native struck Cook from behind with a club, and he fell on his knees. Another stabbed him between the shoulders with a dagger, and he sprawled face down into the shallow water at the sea's edge. A great shout arose, and the crowd flung itself on the captain's body, stabbing in a frenzy of bloodlust.

It was all over quickly. Four Englishmen were killed beside Cook, and the rest scrambled for the nearest boat. Wounded, Phillips was unable to swim, yet he jumped out to help one of his men aboard. Once both boats were out of the way, the big guns of the *Discovery* and the *Resolution* quickly cleared the beach of natives. By then, Cook's body had been dragged away. "When we saw his blood running and heard his groans," so ran a Hawaiian legend, "we said, 'This is not Rono.'"

Only an hour had passed since Cook and his men had gone ashore. And now Cook was dead. He was fifty years old. The men on the *Resolution* and the *Discovery* were quiet that day. Phillips could not put into words how the loss of Cook was lamented; "much less," he wrote, "shall I attempt to paint the horror with which we were struck and the universal dejection which followed so dreadful . . . a calamity."

The Hawaiians too felt mournful - and repentant soon after the episode was over. They had grown to respect Cook, aside from their belief that he was one of their gods. His body was placed on a burning pyre and accorded funeral rites that were usually reserved for the islanders' most revered heroes.

Two days after Cook's death, a native who had shown himself to be a friend of the English delivered a bundle to the *Resolution*. Inside a fine new cloth, and covered with a cloak of black and white feathers, was all that was left of Captain James Cook. It was, according to Captain Charles Clerke, "a large piece of Flesh which we soon saw to be Human and which he gave us to understand was part of the Corpse of our late unfortunate Captain. . . . it was clearly a part of the Thigh, about 6 or 8 pounds without any bone at all – the poor fellow told us that all the rest of the Flesh had been burnt at different places with some peculiar kind of ceremony."

The remains were placed in a coffin, and at sunset on February 21, as the ships' guns boomed a ten-minute salute, the coffin was lowered into the sea. "We all felt we had lost a father," said one seaman. Even the Hawaiian king, Terreeoboo, mourned the death of the English captain, right along with the crew.

With Cook gone, Clerke became leader of the expedition, responsible for guiding the ships home. But Clerke was not well, having been afflicted with tuberculosis even before he had left England. Though the disease had advanced significantly, he could not begin the homeward voyage yet. He felt compelled to complete what Cook had started and to try, if possible, to locate the northern passage. The day after Cook's funeral, Clerke ordered the two ships to weigh anchor. He took command of the *Resolution* and assigned the *Discovery* to Gore.

Sailing northwest toward Asia, the explorers sighted the Kamchatka peninsula on April 23, and at the harbor of St. Peter and St. Paul (now called Petropavlovsk), they were received cordially by the Russians. They even did some trading in furs. Despite language differences, Clerke managed to convey to his hosts that he wished to send a letter home by land. The letter was eventually delivered to the Admiralty, and England learned of the disaster in Kealakekua Bay eight months before the voyage ended.

On June 13, the ships began their second northward push along the Asiatic coast. Dense fog and the thickening ice floes made sailing hazardous and slow - and ultimately impossible. When the *Resolution* and the *Discovery* were fifteen miles short of the point reached on the first attempt, they were stopped. Clerke realized the hopelessness of sailing farther, as well as the seriousness of his own affliction. He was growing weaker daily. On July 27, he turned his ships back.

Less than a month later, Clerke was dead. He was buried at Petropavlovsk, where the ships dropped anchor on August 24. Now John Gore assumed command of the *Resolution*, and James King took over the *Discovery*.

Gore wanted to sail south along the Japanese coast and survey as much of it as possible, but foul weather prevented this. Savage winds split the worn-out sails of both ships and cut the rotten cordage. Driven away from the shore, the ships ran directly to the European settlement at Macao, where they dropped anchor on December 1, 1779.

While the *Resolution* and the *Discovery* were being refitted, their crews turned a handsome profit trading furs with the Chinese.

In Macao, where they could read European newspapers, Gore and King learned that England's war with its American colonies was not going well. By this time, France had entered the conflict against the English. Though French and American ships had been ordered not to molest the vessels of the Cook expedition, Gore took the precaution of bringing guns up from the holds. He made sure the crews were prepared for any emergency as they swept around the Cape of Good Hope and sailed into the North Atlantic. As a further safeguard, Gore altered his course to the west to avoid the European coast. He was taking no chances on an encounter with the French. After such a long period at sea, neither of his ships was in fighting condition; nor did they have the speed to evade pursuit. Gore guided them around Ireland and Scotland before approaching his final anchorage at Deptford on October 6, 1780.

The voyage had lasted four years and almost three months. During that time, the *Resolution* had lost only four men from illness; three of them - Clerke included - had not been in good health when the voyage began. The *Discovery* returned with its crew intact. By continuing to enforce the dietary discipline initiated by Cook, the officers who succeeded him had maintained the crews' good health. Cook had shown that scurvy need not be a major problem on long voyages. He had not convinced them by charm; rather men had trusted him because of the example he set, and because of his sense of responsibility and unshakable confidence.

Cook's confidence betrayed him in the end. But by then, his work was finished. In eleven years of geographical discovery, he had proved that the Pacific was vaster and more varied than most geographers had imagined. He had shown that the unknown southern continent, if it existed, lay too far south to support life. And his foray in the North Pacific had proved that there was no practicable northern passage through which ships of trade might sail.

The explorers who followed him did not diminish the stature of his achievements. They amplified what he had done, but no one ever surpassed his record. From South America to Australia, from the ice islands of the South Pacific to the fogbound Bering Strait, lay thousands of miles of islands, atolls, and ocean that Cook had charted.

Curiosity made Cook an explorer. Zeal and resolution kept him at his tasks and helped him surmount all obstacles. Precision insured that what he saw was fully and accurately recorded. These were the qualities that made up the man. His legacy was knowledge; his monument is the map of the Pacific.

SOURCES

J. C. Beaglehole, *The Exploration of the Pacific* (London, England: Black, 1934).

J. C. Beaglehole, *The Journals of Captain Cook* (Cambridge, England: Cambridge, 1961).

William Bligh, *The Mutiny on Board HMS Bounty* (New York, New York: Signet, 1962).

James Duggard, *Farther Than Any Man: The Rise and Fall of Captain James Cook* (New York, New York: Washington Square, 2002).

Richard Hough, *Captain James Cook: A Biography* (New York, New York: Norton, 1997).

Andrew Kippis, *Captain Cook's Voyages* (New York, New York: Knopf, 1924).

Frank McLynn, *Captain Cook: Master of the Seas* (New Haven, Connecticut: Yale, 2011).

Made in the USA
Coppell, TX
02 March 2025